Commando KidZ

the European adventure

Book Two

Young adult/teen

Fiction/Action-Adventure

Story by: Brenda Elkin

Written by: Brenda Elkin

Commando KidZ ®

Dedicated to my Goddaughters
Gretchen and Kayleigh

Chapter One

I don't care who you are, 4 AM comes early for anyone. So, when the phone rang and vibrated itself off my nightstand, I wasn't happy. But the caller ID gives me a heads up "US government."

"Oh great, don't these people ever sleep," I said reaching down, grabbing the phone off the fake polar bear rug adjacent to my bed.

However, after the third ring, I figured I better answer, so they didn't disperse a seal team to do a welfare check.

"Hello?" I answered, wiping the lingering sleep from my eyes.

"Brenda, how are you?" the familiar voice said, echoing through the loudspeaker.

"Fine, minus the fact I was woken up by a phone call at 4 AM."

"Yes, but when you work for us you work on our dime and our time. There's been a change of plans, the kid's current handler has decided to take a hiatus. So, until further notice, you will take over that position."

"I'm sorry, I guess I must not be awake yet because it sounded like you just said that I'll be in charge of missions."

"That is correct, if we didn't have the utmost confidence you could handle it, for obvious reasons we wouldn't present it."

"Yes, I can understand that, however, Tom is a hardened battlefield veteran. I, however, am a stay-at-home mother of two that has trouble changing batteries in a smoke detector."

"You'll be fine, as I said if we didn't have the utmost confidence, I assure you we would not be sending you out in the field with two of our most valuable juvenile agents. Now, your next mission requires you to be ready and outside of your home in exactly 37 minutes."

"Thirty-seven minutes, you guys really narrow it down to the second don't you. So, where exactly are we going, it's not some barren wasteland in the middle of the Mojave Desert is it?"

"No, it's Europe. We have reliable information that a Russian spy ring, a.k.a. Papa Bear, is operating in and around Paris and Berlin. It's going to be your job, to find out who the leader is and apprehend them for prosecution."

Bizarrely, after receiving the details of our mission, I calmly ended the call and proceeded to wake up Emma and Eric. And I'm glad I did because at the 36 minutes mark a caravan of Humvees pulled into our driveway.

After waiting many hours in the airport lobby, after seeing Eric to his flight, our plane was finally ready at gate 64. I took one last look at where we had been sitting for the past two hours. As Emma and I walked towards the plane, I thought about all the terrible things, the accidents that have been popping up recently on the news.

Once we boarded the plane and tucked ourselves comfortably into the seats, it started its journey toward the runway. Pushing the giant 777, away from its gate the white and blue pilot truck driver jumped out and quickly unlatched the front wheel of the aircraft from its tow bar.

"Hey, Mom? Why do they have to go down this long road, before they take off?" Emma asked.

"They have to build up enough speed. That's why to do that they have to have a lot of distance."

Emma noticed the weather-worn red and white striped windsock hanging from a 20-foot pole just off to the right of the plane next to the runway. Of course, her curiosity piqued. "What's that?" she asked, pointing at the flailing fabric.

"It's a windsock, it helps the pilots. It tells them which direction the wind is blowing, for taking off," I replied, noticing Emma's excitement.

"I wouldn't mind jumping out of a plane again, too bad Eric's not around," Emma said, giggling as she stared out at the rain soaked runway.

"What happened up there? if you want to tell me of course, I don't want to pry."

Suddenly, the armrest under Emma's hand began to shake, she was pushed back into her seat as the G forces from the giant Jet Rolls-Royce engines throttled up to full power.

She leaned over to see the tarmac zipping by the window faster and faster. The harmonic, of the repetitive sound of the wheels striking patched potholes, shook the plane, but not violently.

The plane took off and started its trek toward the blue sky when I heard a rumble under my feet. Although I didn't worry as I thought it was just a landing gear retracting back in the plane. But after sitting in our seats for another four long hours, we heard another rumble, but this rumble couldn't be the landing gear.

Suddenly, the sun was replaced by dark clouds, and rain poured on the windows heavily scratched up.

"Hey, there folks. There is a thunderstorm happening and we're in the middle of it, so please sit back in your seats and buckle up," said the captain.

I figured there was going to be some turbulence by the unpleasant feeling in the plane. But suddenly, the turbulence was so strong that we were almost ripped out of our seats. After a minute or two, however, the turbulence came to an end and the crew on the plane began to carry out food.

But Emma's face was flushed, and ever since she was a little, I knew that look, she was about to get sick. "Honey, are you okay?"

"I don't feel good," she said, resting her head on my shoulder, "can I have some seven up?"

Motioning to the stewardess, I situated Emma with a soda and a small glass of ice, hoping it would settle her tummy before dinner was served.

My food on the plane was a tragedy. I was eagerly waiting for the first meal although the food served on flights is typically low-quality and tasteless.

But they were always the perfect way for me to avoid boredom. The temperature inside the aircraft was so poor that I believe the aircraft was designed to carry frozen meat across the Atlantic Ocean, not human passengers.

It was the middle of the summer, so I didn't have any warm clothing with me. I asked the staff for a blanket, but she explained that they were running out. Right after she was gone, the flight attendants began to transfer blue plastic trays to the trolley. Each tray included a plastic plate, a slice of bread, a yogurt cup, and a bottle of water.

I opened the plastic plate cover, loving its warmth. Then I took a long look inside, inside was white rice and some green curry. Oh, at least it didn't look odd! It seems that the mixture was made of vegetables and there were small bits of chicken and potato in it. Finally, I concluded that temperature-bearing was better than consuming food.

I must've fallen asleep after the atrocious meal because the next thing I knew, I was shaken awake by an ear-splitting "BANG!"

However, the cabin quickly returned to normal. The resonating sounds of the engines and random chatter were all that could be heard. But as I lifted the shade next to Emma's head, a thick trail of black smoke spewed from one of the giant jet engines reverse thruster shield. Although the pilot still hadn't announced an emergency, it was obvious we were having one.

The two flight attendants that had originally greeted us when we boarded, scurried by us, each holding looks of terror on their faces and headed to the back of the plane. Of course, my curiosity being as it is, I needed to find out what was going on and if there was any reason for us to worry.

"Ma'am, you need to take your seat," the first woman said, before turning her attention back to her co-worker who was shaken.

"Excuse me, what was that noise and why hasn't the captain made an announcement?" I asked, staring back at the woman with conviction.

"Ma'am, please return to your seat there's nothing you can do," the second woman, bearing the name tag Helga replied.

"Do? Do about what? Look, if my daughter's life is on the line, I want to know, and I want to know right now!"

"We lost communication with the cockpit. We're not sure what happened, but if I had to guess, I'd say we hit something."

Yet, when I glanced out the window, I saw the cloud cover below us. "How is that possible, birds can fly at this altitude we have to be 30,000," I said.

The flight attendants glanced at each other and whispered amongst themselves. "We don't know if anyone is flying the plane," Helga said, tearing up.

Suddenly, a passenger shouted. "Nobody is flying the plane. What happened to the pilots?" he asked as he had been eavesdropping on their conversation.

"Well, we can't just stand here, my daughter is on this plane."

"Ever since 9/11, all of the cockpit doors have been reinforced. It would take a battering ram to get through it."

"Have you ever heard of the term work smarter, not harder?" I quickly walked back to my seat and felt Emma's forehead. It was cool to the touch, so I was confident she didn't have a bug. "Sweetheart, how do you feel?"

"Okay, I guess what was that noise?" she asked, sitting up exposing her care bears sweatshirt.

"Honey, do you feel up to picking a lock?"

Emma's eyes lit up. "Really?" she asked.

I reached down, picked her up, and then started my journey back to re-join the stewardesses. I'm glad it was a short distance because Emma was no longer the meager 10 pounds she used to be when I toted her everywhere with me.

"Ladies, this is my daughter Emma. She is a world-class locksmith, so far up to date she has not come across the lock she is not been able to pick. You said it would take a battering ram to go through the door, why not just let her open it?"

The women hesitated for a moment and gave each other a stare, but then began whispering to each other. This of course was trying my patience because when I looked out the window just by the cloud cover, I could see our altitude dropping. This could only mean the pilots were not in control of the aircraft as we were now over the Atlantic Ocean with no land in sight.

"What do you need from us?" Helga asked, leading us to the cockpit door.

"I have to see the lock, it'll give me a better idea of what I'm dealing with, but if it's something homeland security or the FAA designed, it should be as simple as playing with my Legos."

"Confident little girl, isn't she," Helga said, with a smile, taking Emma by the hand and showing her the lock next to a keypad.

The door was gray metal covered by a thin coat of laminate. It looks heavy-duty in nature and intimidating by sight. In the center of the door, just a few inches from the handle resided a half a dollar-sized keyhole, with three tiers of brass that held six copper tumblers. It was designed to reset if someone tried to pick it, or alter it in any way. Emma was more than aware of this feature but showed no apprehension when faced with it.

Although, one thing did flood her mind, the keypad, because if it was linked to the tumblers, it could electronically reset every time she got one in place. But she didn't find discouragement in this possibility, she found a challenge.

"I need a pen, a bobby pin, and something with carbonation, a soda, champagne."

The plastic tubing from the ballpoint pen would be used as a buffer, and the bobby pin would be used as the driver that would pop each tumbler. The carbonation, from the beverages, would help divert the signal from the keypad. This would give her the extra time she figured she may need so it wouldn't reset after each sequence.

Another stewardess who appeared from first-class carried an, uncorked bottle of Dom Perignon while the woman behind her had a handful of unopened Coca-Cola and Pepsi cans. Suddenly, our ears popped, warning us that we were losing altitude.

I handed Emma the pen I had stashed away in my purse, she quickly took it apart and pulled out the plastic tubing that held the ink inside.

"When I tell you to," she said to the woman holding the champagne, "I want you to pour the champagne on the keypad, but not until I tell you to, okay."

The terrified woman nodded three times in compliance, popping the cork on the bottle.

Slowly, Emma's tiny hand maneuvered the bobby pin that one of the stewardesses had gotten through the keyhole from a passenger. Her father used to say that picking locks were a lot like fishing. He'd say, "When you strike the first tumbler, it's like hooking a 600-pound Marlin. There's nothing like it."

Within no time, Emma's competence paid off as she popped the first and second tumbler into their housing, but hesitated before she went to the third one. "Okay, I'm gonna count to three, and then I want you to pour it on to the keypad. One, two."

"Emma wait, something's wrong," I said, licking the tips of my fingers before running them along the seal of the cockpit door. I could feel the air, cold chilled air not like the ambient climate-controlled air in the cabin that was currently at 75°.

"What's wrong, why did you stop her?" one of the stewardesses asked.

Chapter Two

"I'm not sure, but there shouldn't be this much air blowing in from the cockpit. That's not a good sign," I finished, looking down at Emma still crouching down by the lock.

"Mom, what should we do?" Emma asked, getting to her feet.

"We need to get as many shirts and blankets as possible and fashion them into a rope. We can anchor them to the base of the chairs in first-class."

After another arduous 10 minutes, the passengers and crew worked together to make too long strands about 50 feet apiece. They tied them off to the base of two empty chairs in first-class and the other ends to our waists.

"Emma, as soon as the door opens, move over towards the coffee pots as quickly as possible because if the windshield is gone, the suction will pull you right out of the plane. You need to tell everyone to put their seatbelts on because I have a feeling it's going to get windy in here pretty quick. And for God's sake if anybody has anything on their laps or tray tables secure it. We don't need any projectiles, all right?"

The stewardesses scattered throughout the cabin of the plane collecting trash and instructing the passengers to close and lock all tray tables. Others made announcements over the PA, warning travelers to make sure their seatbelts were secured. Finally, the moment of truth arrived, I wasn't as concerned about what was behind the door as I was for my daughter safety. But as the woman handed me the bottle of champagne, and I inched my way closer to the keypad I knew there was no turning back and simply nodded at Emma.

After rifling with the lock for a couple of moments, Emma leaned her head back and made eye contact. "Okay Mom, here we go one, two, three, pour it, Mom."

Suddenly, there was a "BUZZ, CLANK, CLINK, CLINK," but before the sound stopped, a large metal door swung inward with such force, it caused a large dent in the navigator's seat that was set directly behind it. The massive rush of air proved my prediction right as the windshield was indeed gone. There were no pilots to be found, and the navigator's area was empty. Emma was quickly lifted off the floor but didn't seem to mind as her blonde hair smacked her in the face, and she gripped a hold of the wall to steady herself.

The massive rush of wind made it hard to breathe, so we had to turn our heads to the side to inhale as it was virtually impossible to do it facing forward. I reached the pilot's chair and somehow managed to pull myself in, holding myself in place with my knees pressed up against the instrument panel. I locked the five-point harness around my chest and torso before reaching over and pulling Emma down into the co-pilot's seat, keeping my arm around her waist until she snapped her straps into place.

I pulled the headset back in that was swinging wildly in the wind outside the cockpit window. After checking it for damage, I flipped on the Satcom switch above my chair, and called out an emergency. "Mayday, Mayday, Mayday. We have an emergency, Mayday, Mayday, Mayday. We are on a passenger jet flying over the Atlantic are pilots are missing, and the windshield is gone I repeat the windshield is gone."

It seemed like an eternity had passed before the Satcom crackled to life. "Heavy 379 this is Heathrow airport. What seems to be the nature of your emergency? Over," the man asked in a thick Manchester accent.

"I'm not sure tower, but we're losing altitude, and as I said we have no pilots."

"Do you have any flying experience, with any type of aircraft? Over."

"No, I do not, but if we don't do something soon, we are going to be getting wet," I said, trying to hold back a desperate tone.

"All right, let's just take a deep breath and we will walk you through this, all right. These planes are state of the art. If need be they could land them bloody selves, so no worries. Now the first thing we're going to have you do is you must look for the autopilot. Assuming you're where your transponder shows you are, it should be engaged. It's going to be a red button on the left-hand side of your console. Do you see it, love?" the senior tower controller asked.

I search the console diligently until I found the button he was referring to and pushed it. Of course, this brought on a whole new set of problems. I heard a voice through my headphones announce, "autopilot disengaged," a millisecond before the nose of the aircraft sharply pointed itself to the glassy ridged waves thousands of feet below us. The panel lit up like a Christmas tree, and an alarm broadcasted that we were losing altitude.

Somehow, I knew to grab the steering column and gently pull it back until the nose of the plane was horizontal again.

"Heavy 379, did you disengage the autopilot? Over."

"Yes Heathrow, I did but she took a sharp dive, so I pulled back on the stick. I got her leveled off now, and the altimeter says we are at 27,000 feet but still dropping."

"Roger that heavy 379, well, unfortunately, there are no floating airports in your vicinity. So, you're going to have to land the old girl. Over."

"Mom, do you know how to fly a plane?" Emma asked, her eyes watering so badly it looked as if she was crying.

"I don't think so, honey. But right now, we don't have a lot of other options. Just help me keep an eye on our altitude, it's going to be on the left-hand side of your screen near the top. It will say altimeter, do you see it."

She nodded in acknowledgment and turned her attention back to it.

"Heavy 379, how are things going, any problems? Over."

"Negative Heathrow, just trying to figure out if it will make it because I see no land anywhere, just miles and miles of water."

"Roger that heavy 379, but you are closer than you think, however, you will need to turn the aircraft just slightly to the north. Currently, your heading should be 1175, but you needed to be 1180. You're going to have a keypad on your screen, that will say LAS/LOC. This is your location transmitter, it controls your navigation and your flight path. Do you see the keyboard on your screen? Over."

"Um... Yes, I see it."

"Brilliant, now on the keypad, you're going to type in 1180 and then press enter. Over."

"Okay, I did it. But nothing seems to be happening, were not turning or anything."

"That's all right, don't worry. Now, you're going to reengage the autopilot, the computer in the plane will recognize the new coordinates. After that, she should fly herself right to our back door. Over."

"Okay, how do I do that, reengage the autopilot?"

"All right, it's very simple just look for the button I told you about on the right-hand side, and press it again. This should reengage the autopilot, now once this happens, you're going to want to let go of the stick and keep your feet off the pedals that are just below the cockpit. Over."

"I pressed it. The plane is turning but we're still losing altitude. Currently, we're at 21,000 feet."

"What's your airspeed love, it will be on your screen on the right-hand side?"

"It says 340 knots, now it's 339. It's dropping fast, should it be doing that?" I asked, holding back my fear.

"Heavy 379. Yes, it's completely normal. The plane's computer will determine the proper speed. Now, very shortly you should have a visual on Heathrow. She's a big girl, do you see her lights yet? Over."

"Not yet, oh wait... I see them now. But the plane's not turning towards them, is that normal?"

"Heavy 379. Yes, it is, what is your current altitude? You should be at 14,000 feet. Over."

"Um... Yes, we are at 14,000 feet exactly. Wait... I hear a noise, coming from the belly of the plane, sounds like a buzzing sound."

"Heavy 379. That's all right, it should be your flaps and ailerons, the old girl's just stretching her legs and getting ready to land, nothing to worry yourself about. What is your altitude currently? Over."

"Ten thousand one hundred feet, there's another sound, this one is louder, and it's making a clunking sound."

"Heavy 379. That would be your landing gear, now you're going to want to make sure the front of our craft is going to be lined up with runway 54, again that's runway 54."

My eyes at this point were watering so badly from the blasting wall of wind protruding through the gaping hole in the fuselage, I could barely see. But what I could, was enough to scare me beyond my wildest nightmares, the ground and it's coming up fast. As the runway lights got closer, so did the fear of crashing.

"Heavy 379. Now, here comes the fun part, do you see the two pedals down by your feet? As soon as her wheels touchdown on the tarmac, you're going to want to push on those pedals as hard as you possibly can, all right? Over."

"Why, what do the petals do, are they like breaks or something?" I asked, reluctant to touch them with my feet.

"Heavy 379. That is correct, they'll help stop your roll. But you must keep them depressed until the engines wind down because even at a quarter of acceleration, they will still have enough thrust to push the plane off the runway. And we don't want that now do we, all right love, we see you on the horizon. You're looking good, just remember what I said, as soon as you touchdown get up on those bloody things and push with all your might. All right, here we go, you're at 5000, 4500, 3000, 2000, 1000, 500, 200. All right love get ready you're going to make contact in five, four, three, two, one. Contact! Push, push, push, push, push, push, push!"

The once intimidating roar from the massive jet engines quickly got muffled. But as we passed multiple yellow emergency vehicles on each side of the plane, I realized how serious the situation was and stood fast on the 7 1/2-inch metal pedals under the console until the gigantic aircraft came to a slow stop within just a few feet of the end of the runway.

Of course, unbeknownst to me, during this entire emergency, the pilots who had been sucked out of the cockpit had gotten their uniforms snagged on the broken glass and were miraculously still alive. They were tended to by the emergency crews waiting close by to my relief. But with little fanfare, our English co-parts whisked us away from the airport to a hotel not far away.

"Okay, Mom that was pretty cool," Emma said with a smile, before closing the bathroom door.

As our driver zipped through the cobblestones streets and turned into the first roundabout, Big Ben sat off to our right.

London is the capital and the largest city in Britain. It is situated on the south side of the Thames, with a population of around 8.4 million, of which 2.7 million live in the inner London neighborhoods.

According to 2012 figures, its total population in all its suburbs is approximately 15,010,295 inhabitants. This is Europe's largest city by population and one of the most important cultural, political, and economic hubs in Europe.

Tourism in London is ideal for all ages, young and old as well as all nationalities, with restaurants offering traditional meals from around the world, often in public parks.

There's also a popular market on the southern side of the River Thames called Burro Market, as well as other commercial markets that include the world's most famous restaurants and shops, particularly clothes, jewelry, and handicraft shops line the city's east Brick Lane Street.

London is also popular for the Camden market on the north side and the Portobello Road on the west side. To enjoy shopping, it's easier to stroll to these markets where you can see colorful houses and shops selling old crafts on the street leading to the market.

"Mom, what's that, is that Big Ben?"

"It sure is, Big Ben is the term for the striking clock's Great Bell at the north end of London's Westminster Palace, which is generally generalized to refer to both the clock and clock tower. The tower's official name in which Big Ben is situated was originally the Clock Tower; it was renamed Elizabeth Tower in 2012 to mark Queen Elizabeth II's Diamond Jubilee, United Kingdom."

"Why is it there, and so big?"

Possibly London's most famous landmark, this clock tower stands above the Houses of Parliament, the former site of Westminster Palace. Though the tower has long been named "Big Ben," it actually belongs to the tower's largest bell, weighing over 13 tons. The tower is 320 feet high itself, with four clock faces, 23 feet across each. The tower, however, you want to refer to it, is a striking subject for parliament houses, particularly when the sun throws the entire structure into golden relief. The entire complex is overflowing with history, from Guy Fawkes gunpowder plot to the world's oldest democracy site.

"Well, Big Ben is the symbol of the British Parliament and one of the world's most accurate clocks. If the chimes are off by even two seconds a year, it's making the 5 o'clock news. Big Ben is also an outstanding London landmark of considerable architectural significance."

Then as we turned toward Westminster Abby, the Tower of London came into our view. Historically, the buildings and grounds acted as a royal residence, a political fortress, a place of execution, an arsenal, a royal mint, a menagerie, and a public record office. It is situated on the north side of the River Thames in the extreme western part of the Tower Hamlets area, on the border with central London.

"What's that Mom?" Emma said pointing at the centuries-old building.

"Well, the Tower of London, formerly her Majesty's Royal Palace and the Tower of London Fortress, is a medieval castle on the north bank of the River Thames in central London. It is situated in the London Borough of Tower Hamlets which is divided from the eastern edge of the square mile of the City of London by the vast expanse known as Tower Hill. It was created at the end of 1066 as part of the Norman Conquest of England."

"Wow, really that's awesome. Can we go, do they have tours?" Emma said, pressing her nose against the glass in the backseat of the meticulously maintained Bentley.

The driver, a middle-aged English man named Ian, with a heavy Manchester accent took a little-known service road to the left of Westminster Abbey. The expansive English countryside, when on as far as the eye could see, before they pulled up to a gate, that was more heavily guarded in the last two they had passed through.

Another well-dressed man donning a suit and tie approached our car. "Good afternoon ladies. If you would be so kind as to follow me," he announced, waiting for us to exit.

Chapter Three

"What? Are we meeting with the Queen, or is this the normal greeting for Americans?" I said, attempting to add levity to the already tense situation.

"Oh, American humor, oh well, Bob's your uncle?"

"What does 'Bob's your uncle' mean?" Emma asked, spinning around 360° to get a full-on view of the architectural spectacle that surrounded them.

"Oh, I guess if I had to translate, it would be 'whatever' or 'okay.' So, no worries."

Walking into the large cathedral, our mouths dropped, the towering ceiling hundreds of feet over our head was crisp and detailed. The pews were immaculate, as were the stained-glass windows that invited sunlight into the old church. The car-sized pipe organ that took up half the altar sat quiet and dormant but it's polished brass tubes, and piping still caught our attention.

"Do you play that, on Sundays, or is it just for looks?" Emma asked, approaching the behemoth musical instrument.

"Every morning at 6 AM, Mrs. Crabapple tickles the ivories, as they say, just to keep it in tune, of course, Sunday mass is when it gets its most use. Nevertheless, watch your step," he said, holding open two confessional doors sitting towards the back of the church, "in you go," he added, closing our doors simultaneously after we had entered.

"Mom, what's happening? Why are we in these confessionals," Emily said, just before the floor dropped out and we were whisked down a series of tubes before coming to a gentle stop in our capsules.

Our doors opened up with a "whoosh." Immediately after, we were met by two men and a woman wearing Royal Air Force uniforms.

"Welcome to MI6," the woman announced, "my name is agent Montgomery. Would you like a cup of tea before we get started?"

"I'll take some hot chocolate," Emma replied, bypassing her host's offer of tea.

Playing in the background, but at a comfortable tone was Sebastian Bach's fourth symphony in a minor adding a touch of elegance to our current environment. We were led down along a well-lit hallway, that was riddled with pictures of Queen Elizabeth and Queen Mary.

Suddenly, agent Montgomery placed her hand on a device built into the wall and was met by a male English voice. "Fingerprint scan complete, access granted. Good afternoon agent Montgomery."

"This," she said, leading us into an airplane hangar-sized room that was a chaotic circus of movement and sound, "is the heart and soul of MI6. Our eyes reach across the globe, at any given minute we know what's happening in downtown London as well as Perth Australia. We have satellites trained on every country in the world, including the United States."

"I thought the United States and England were allies, how come you watch us?" Emma asked, brushing her blonde hair from her eyes.

"We are popping, but you must admit you yanks are a bit like a bull walking through a nitroglycerin factory. We never know what you're going to do and say next, so we keep our ears to the ground."

"I think the United States is the greatest country on earth," I said, getting defensive.

"Oh, I meant no disrespect. It's just here across the pond, we view things slightly differently than you. That's all, let's keep moving, we've got a lot to do and very little time to do it."

"Thank you, agent Montgomery, that will be all," a portly English man in a blue suit with a checkered vest said, before shaking our hands, and leading us into a large well-lit conference room with a long table situated in the middle. "Please, have a seat," he said, gesturing to the chairs pushed up against the wall.

"Knock, knock! Excuse me, director, here you go dear," an old woman with blue hair and round-framed glasses said, handing Emma her hot chocolate before quickly exiting the room.

"This is so good," Emma said, "taste like it was ripped straight out of Willy Wonka's chocolate river."

"Yes, we certainly enjoy it. Back to business, in 2010 we were made aware of a program that it been started by the Russian government that was very similar to the ones you have in the USA. They trained these juvenile delinquents, and then send them off to private schools that some of the most important children in the world attend."

"Why would they do that?" Emma asked, repeatedly taking small sips of her chocolatey beverage.

"The children they befriend. Their parents are world leaders, dictators, and ambassadors, all high-ranking government officials. Unfortunately, they know all of our counterspies and that's where you come in, we need you to infiltrate the little sec and relay back as much information as possible. We believe that the former KGB is attempting to hire Al Qaeda insurgents to detonate a dirty bomb at the meeting on the 23rd at the United Nations."

"I'm not sure how we can help, they haven't really given us high-quality training," I said, using air quotes.

"Sixty-seven minutes ago you landed a jumbo jet, with over 200 passengers on it. So, they must've done something right or you wouldn't be sitting here would you."

I hate to admit it, but after 45 minutes of listening to the low toned and dull voice emanating from the director, I nodded off. I couldn't help it, between the stress on the flight and everything else, I was exhausted, and I could tell Emma wasn't faring much better.

"In 1941, the German government began development on a project named MorningStar. It was essentially the first program to design a nuclear arsenal. By 1942, our allies realize this and later found it had come to fruition. However, after the end of World War II, the facility rumored to be under the city of Berlin was never located. At least by us."

I was almost afraid to ask, as I sat there twiddling my thumbs staring at the cage clock above the door well. But after what seemed like an eternity had passed, I couldn't take it anymore and spoke up. "You want us, to find a nuclear bomb?"

"Um... Yes," the director said, in a presumptive tone.

"Okay, let's pump the brakes. I have my child with me, and I am not taking her anywhere near a bomb. So, you can call our contacts and tell them no deal."

"Surely, they must have to give you some type of insight, they couldn't have sent you here blind."

"They never said anything Prince Charles, and I'm not real thrilled with your belittling tone."

"So, did you think they sent you here on vacation, use your bloody brain for puff sake."

However, breaking the tension, and without warning, Emma stood up and kicked the director in the groin causing him to buckle over and almost fall to the ground. "Don't talk to my mother like that," she yelled, holding her stance she had learned in karate!

"Bloody Hell," the director stuttered, trying to catch his breath.

"Emma! Sit down! When we get home, you're grounded young lady," I said, holding back my laughter.

"I apologize, director. My daughter has a bit of a short temper. Are you okay?" I asked, but I could see his bright cherry red face in the drool seeping from one side of his cheek and down his chin.

Fifteen minutes had passed before he got to his feet, occasionally still buckling over, to grab his stomach. He found his way to a chair and sat back, rocking randomly back and forth while mumbling what I could only perceive to be English swearwords under his breath.

"Can you please keep your offspring restrained, whilst you're here," were the director's only words for the next few minutes while he attempted to regain his composure?

"Again, I am terribly sorry. She never does that, but yes I will keep her under control," I said attempting to stay straight faced, but apparently, my efforts weren't valiant enough.

"I don't think it's very funny, kicking a man in his dingleberries. Frankly, it's quite rude!"

Looking over at Emma, I gave her a wink and tried to assure her I wasn't really angry. Yet after almost 30 minutes, the director didn't seem to recover and beckoned for agent Montgomery. The stout English woman dressed in a navy-blue pantsuit with multiple IDs hanging from the front pocket gestured us to follow her down along the door with a hallway.

Abruptly, she waved her hand in front of what appeared to be a nondescript concrete wall that was painted white. Suddenly, two doors slid open with a 'whoosh.' "Follow me, please," she said, stepping into the elevator.

We must've gone another 500 feet underground before the elevator stopped with the 'ding.' Exiting, we followed her to the end of another hallway, but this one had a set of white metal doors and a yellow flashing strobe light directly at the end of it. Bizarrely, the air smelled like electricity, the kind you would only get by using an ionization machine, so I figured whatever we were about to see was going to be fantastic.

"This is our weapons laboratory; you may recognize some of the employees."

"ERIC!" Emily yelled, running over to greet her brother with a tight hug.

"How did you, get here before us, they said at the airport you were going to Australia?"

"Oh, he will be, but we figured would bring him over first, he seems to have a brilliant understanding of plasma energy. Surprisingly, more in-depth than our scientists, so tit-for-tat. Master Eric, would you care to show your mum what you helped come up with?" agent Montgomery asked, leaning back against the cabinet with arms crossed.

"Sure. So, this is what they call a 'Truth-All.' It carries a very heavy positive magnetic charge that wreaks havoc on the nervous system and scrambles the neural signals in the brain. Allowing them, to only communicate the first thought that comes to mind. Which would be what they're trying to hide. It has a 99.8% success rate. And of course, it's nonlethal."

"But it looks like just a strip of metal, how can something so small do that?" Emma questioned, taking a sample from her brother's hand.

"It's just positively charged, there are no other working components. You just place it around someone's wrist like this," Eric said, clamping the piece of formidable metal around Emily's wrist, "and then just ask them a question." "Hey, M did you eat all of my jellybeans that Nana gave me last year, or did the dog really eat them?"

"I ate them and threw up. Mom's spaghetti isn't what got me sick," Emma admitted, involuntarily. Then grabbed the device off her wrist, adding, "I don't like this one."

"Next, we have the censoring-trans-magnetic-plasma-pulse gun or 'STOP' for short. It's very similar to the type of stun gun law enforcement utilizes, except for one very important feature... It allows you to keep your suspect immobilized for up to six hours with just one application. Don't worry, M. I am not going to use this on you, I've seen what it does, they let me test it on an agent. He's still walking funny," Eric announced, placing the shiny aluminum plated nonlethal weapon back on the brightly lit display table.

I know that parents always brag about their children's accolades and achievements, but this was blowing my mind. Watching my firstborn display a host of nonlethal weapons, that he apparently had a hand in designing, was breath-taking because I'd always known since day one, he was gifted. This was simply just another way of confirming that, I don't think I could've been any prouder as I sat there beaming. However, interrupting my train of thought was the rumbling of my stomach, reminding me of the horrific food on the flight.

But I didn't want to interrupt, so I wrapped my arms around my stomach, in hopes of muffling it.

"I am so proud of you Eric," I said, trying to contain my mom feelings.

"Thanks, Mom, next we have 'semi-organic-orbital-translocation-transponder or what I call 'SPOT.' The reason I named it that is because of these little round balls," he said, exposing three one inch metallic-looking spheres resting in the palm of his hand.

"They look like paintballs, what's so special about that, you can go to any arcade and rent them," Emma quipped, giving her brother ribbing,

"They contain a semi-organic material and fully operational nanobots. They can be tracked through any obstacle or material including up to 500 feet underground or underwater. They were designed to assist in emergency extractions. So, no matter where you are, you simply shoot one of the projectiles at the target and presto they hone in on the signal."

"That's remarkable Eric, what made you think of this honey?" I asked, getting up from my chair to take a closer look.

"Well, every time you see a spy movie, there's always that one place that a signal can't get through, whether it's in a concrete bunker, or a basement of some creepy mansion and never have enough power. So, rather than ramping up the power source, I looked outside the box, because the nanobots can be programmed to find one another."

"You mean like how worker bees locate their Queen?" I asked, gently removing one of the spheres as not to damage it from Eric's hand.

"Exactly, except these are only semi-organic based so they're not able to put out the pheromone that bees rely on, but the artificial signal is very similar."

"It's really remarkable son, I'm so proud of you. I'm so proud of both of you."

"Nothing like a mother's love," agent Montgomery said, and at first sound startling the trio.

"Oh, I'm sorry agent, you were so quiet we forgot you were here."

"No worries, but you're right to be proud. This lad has helped us more in six months, than our entire Advanced Technology team has in the last five years. Eric's insight on plasma storage and diffusion is the reason this is possible. He has been an indispensable asset, he even gained the Queen's approval, which I'm sure you know is rare in itself."

"The last thing I have, which I'm very proud of might I add is a gigawatt laser-assisted systems scanner or 'Glass,' here M," Eric said, handing his sister the 3 x 6" long transparent device disguised as a random piece of glass.

"It looks like a windowpane out of Grandpa's old greenhouse," Emily said, examining the seemingly useless apparatus.

"Place your thumb on the right-hand corner," Eric said, waiting for his sister's opinion to change.

Of course, as soon as his sister did as he requested, the clear piece of glass lit up into a small computer screen. With the Google logo rotating at the top of the screen, followed by a banner that read 'Welcome Emma to the World Wide Web, how may we assist.'

Chapter Four

"Oh my God, Eric! This is incredible, it's so thin when it was off, I thought it was a piece of glass or plastic or something. If you wouldn't have told us what it was, I would've never guessed in a million years," I said, taking it from Emma's hands to examine it. But suddenly the screen went blank. "I didn't break it did I?" I asked Eric.

"No, it's only programmed for Emma's fingerprint. It was too difficult to line up multiple security parameters. So, I figured since she's more computer savvy than you are, I just make it hers because you have to admit Mom you are not great on a keyboard."

"Oh, I get it, trust me I know, you know when I was a kid, our telephones were meant for making phone calls. Just thought I'd throw that out there."

"Yes Mom, we know back in your day you had to read by candlelight because electricity hadn't been invented yet."

"Hey! How old do you think I am, and we had electricity. Heck, we even had a color TV, so I'm not that ancient."

"Oh brother," Emma remarked, rolling her eyes.

"Yes, I hate to interrupt the family reunion, but time is of the essence," agent Montgomery said, tapping on her wristwatch. "Maybe we should scurry along, hmm?"

I looked up at the cage clock still hanging above the door, three hours had gone by, and I was hungry and tired, so I could imagine how Emma was feeling. We set for another 60 minutes, pushing through Eric's presentation before agent Montgomery announced we had to be fitted for night vision goggles, and body armor, so we would need to go to another room. The facility was as large as three aircraft hangars, about 30,000 ft.², of course, mind you this was only an estimate, but it was massive in size with multiple floors and levels.

"Excuse me, my daughter and I have an ate since yesterday, is there any chance we can get something to eat before we continue?"

"Surely, you must be kidding I thought that we'd given you a bite upstairs?"

But as neither Emma nor I confirmed this, agent Montgomery said she would have none of it. Walking us to what appeared to be a cafeteria, she instructed us to order anything we desired as it was compliments of MI6.

Embarrassed to say, I gorged myself on the English cuisine, rather enjoying my bangers and mash. Which to the layman is simply sausage and hash browns, but it was enough to stop the hunger pains I'd become accustomed to over the last hour. The room bustled with activity, neatly dressed agents entered and exited hastily after receiving their food from the server. We sat for an hour, going over the day's events and explaining to Eric our close call at 30,000 feet, before being rushed off to the next location.

After traversing a spider web of hallways, we entered a laboratory. It was filled with so many neon vivid colors that its toxic, bright tube lights was why there was not one unlit corner. The room was scattered with lab equipment, Bunsen burners and test tubes were littered about the clearly worn countertops. White cabinets lined the walls, punctuated by floor to ceiling glass cases that display a combination of equipment. A fume hood lurked in one corner of the room and the table in front of us had two sinks and a gas hook-up at the center.

Nothing else rested on its surface, the space was immaculate, and you know there was a place for everything, and everything was in its place. Beakers filled with mysterious fluids and substances, and large Kevlar blankets, padded a back wall that clearly had seen better days. It has six to seven-inch chunks of concrete missing from behind it. Dark charred burn marks and tattered and torn holes could be seen on a second sheet hanging up next to it. Making me wonder, what could've done such damage as I was familiar with the durability of Kevlar.

"Now, the premise behind night vision is it amplifies what light exists even if the human eye cannot pick it up. However, if the device does not snugly fit around your head, it doesn't illuminate properly. And in a crack situation, you won't have the luxury of time, to try and readjust it. So, as a preventative, each one of our agents is fitted with formfitting goggles, and what that means is that yours will only fit you because it's designed to fit around your facial features because no one person is identical. All are different in some way, even if it's just slightly. Some have a sloped nose; others might have a narrow chin or dimples. These things have to be taken into consideration. Now the gentleman who does this is Dr. Julian Brubeck, our chief scientific officer."

"Good afternoon ladies, as my colleague mentioned, my name is Dr. Brubeck. What we're going to do today, is set you up with a pattern of night vision goggles or better known as E stats. They will amplify any light in any situation except of course in the water and will allow you the gift of night vision. But it is very important that when you're fitted, you keep your face in a position that it would normally be in, this will prevent any miscalculations in the seal around your eyes. Do you have any questions, anything I may answer?" the old frizzy white-haired man asked in a hard to understand thick English accent while adjusting his pressed white lab coat.

"So, you're like Q in the James Bond movies? That is so cool, can we have a Maserati that turns into a submarine too?" Emma asked, picking things up around the room, to examine them.

"Come again, you know James Bond is make-believe right lassy?"

"She was just kidding Dr., my sister's a real joker. She knows James Bond is make-believe, don't you M," Eric said, pushing Emma's shoulder, as he walked by.

"Yes, I know James Bond is not real. But he's got some cool stuff, you don't by chance have any ballpoint pens that turn into explosive devices, do you?"

"Where did you get this one, is she for real?"

"I'm sorry, my daughter has jet lag, she's not really herself," I said, snapping my fingers at Emma. "You need to stop it," I said in a hushed tone, but still getting her attention.

"The next thing she'll ask is if Alice in Wonderland is real, you yanks. As I was saying, it'll take two hours for it to set. So, we need to get started, all you'll be here all bloody day!"

The harmonic buzz in the room from all of the machines and equipment began to lull me to sleep. I sat just off to the right where Emma had been asked to take a seat, while Dr. Brubeck and his assistant took measurements of her nose and cheeks, chin, and forehead, even measuring the space between her eyes and ears. I could see she was getting fidgety, as her light blue my little pony sneakers swung aimlessly beneath her chair. But a snap of my fingers brought her around, and she stopped squirming.

As I watched her and Eric, I couldn't help but wonder who came up with the program Commando Kidz because frankly, after first being alerted to it I was all against it. But now that I was able to see things a little more clearly, it made more sense.

It not only gave our country the added boost of security it needed, it gave Emma and Eric something their father and I couldn't, competence and stamina. They were able to do things I could've never imagined doing at their age. Emma was now speaking different languages fluently, including Mandarin. And with Eric designing his line of nonlethal weapons, it was just amazing. I think the worst part about it was, it was all so damn clandestine, I couldn't brag to anyone.

"All right, we're ready for you love. My dear, you can get down now, you're all set. We have to do your mum next," the doctor's assistant announced, helping Emma down from the chair.

I could smell the antiseptic and hear a slight buzzing coming from behind me as I pushed back in the heavily padded chair that slightly resembled a barber. The doctor gently pushed my head back and told me to focus on the X painted on the wall directly across from me and not to move while he set the plastic sheet across my eyes and nose.

"All right, it's going to start getting warm, but nothing to worry about, just sit tight we're almost done. There we are, all set. Now, you're each going to receive the weapons your sibling and son describe to you, so don't lose them. The only program to work according to your biometrics. So, for instance, if you lose your 'Truth-all,' and you try to use your mum's it won't work, and that goes both ways. Let's say your mum loses her 'GLASS' she won't be able to use yours because it's only programmed for your fingerprints. Understand?"

"Completely," I said, realizing I would have to keep track of not only mine but Emma's as well. Which I knew, was going to be an issue, she could barely keep track of her shoes when she got home let alone these things.

"Hang tight for a moment, agent Montgomery will be back shortly. She had some urgent business to tend to, but when she comes back, she will give you the specifics of your mission, and the parameters you must follow."

"What do you mean the parameters we have to follow?" I asked, out of naivety.

"Oh, well that's simple. Don't get caught. That's it because if you do, you're on your own, we don't know you. Understand?"

"Why is that, you throw us out to the wolves and then don't acknowledge our existence? That's kinda crappy, we wouldn't do that with you," Emma snapped, which kind of surprised me to be honest.

"Well, I'm sorry popping, we're not running a day-care. If you can't handle yourself in the field, maybe you should go back to kindergarten."

Of course, before the man finished speaking, I knew what my daughter was going to do. But I have to admit, the guy was a pompous ass, and whatever she did to him, I had no issues with.

"Hey, get away from me you little sprite. I'm warning you, OH BLOODY HELL. She hit me in my dingleberries," the doctor's assistant bellowed, rolling back and forth on the floor grabbing his groin.

"For someone who's in special intelligence, you're not very smart. Do you not see my daughter's right at that level? Where do you think she was going to punch first, use your head gentlemen."

After Emma sat down, and Dr. Brubeck's assistant managed to get to his feet and excused himself. Agent Montgomery returned, and let us back down to the same cafeteria we had breakfast in earlier and instructed us to wait there as our new mission head would be joining us shortly. Eric and I didn't have a problem with the local cuisine, Emma on the other hand was a different story. Because my daughter has always been a picky eater, bringing her to another country and trying to get her to eat was like pulling teeth from a conscious lion. Dangerous, and tricky.

"Mom, what's a spotted dick?"

"Oh my God! Emma watch your language. Don't you ever say that again!"

"Hey, Mom. It's a dessert, it's like the sponge cake, it's got icing on top and fruit inside. Like dates, and apples, that kind of stuff," Eric replied, laughing.

"Oh... I... I didn't know that. Oh, yeah it's right up there on the board next to ice cream."

I felt foolish, yes, I'll admit. But hearing my child say, 'spotted dick,' was rather unnerving, even if it was a traditional English dessert.

"Mom, can I try some spotted..."

But I jumped in, and cut her off, "Emma, just have some ice cream. Okay?"

An ear-splitting buzzer sounded above our heads. Agents ran past us looking as if they had a mission of their own and would stop at nothing to complete it. However, when I saw Eric's reaction to the noise and bustling chaos, I started to worry that maybe this was a routine exercise. I reached over to where Emma was standing as she had just stood up to get ice cream and pulled her back close to me whispering to her, "Stay put, I don't know what's going on, you don't want to get underfoot."

Agent Montgomery examined the room and looked at her watch as she talked into it. "HQ, is this a drill?" she asked, making sure to keep her eye on her surroundings.

"Negative agent, this is not a drill. I repeat this is not an exercise. Security has been breached, get the Yanks to bunker 72 at all costs. Shoot to kill agent," the voice on the watch announced loud enough for us to hear before cutting out.

"KEEP YOUR HEADS DOWN AND DO AS I SAY!"

"Mom, what's happening I'm scared?" Emma cried out, crawling into my lap.

"LET'S MOVE OUT! FOLLOW ME!"

"Agent Montgomery, what's happening, what's going on?" I asked, not thinking I would get a response.

"Our security perimeters been breached; the little wankers know you're here. So, we've got to get you out of here and in one piece."

"I'm sorry, was that ever really in question. Getting out in one piece," I said, grabbing Eric by his shirt.

"Well, you know things happen here and there. It's what you'd call a tossup, I mean let's be honest, it's not the safest occupation in the world now is it," agent Montgomery said, pulling her Glock 17 from its side holster, pulling the slide back and loading a bullet in the chamber.

After seeing this, I realized it was no drill, and this woman meant business. I looked over at Eric and Emma, and I could see the fear. But their tenacity was brilliant, and un-wavering even faced with an adrenaline-fueled situation. It was impressive, and I beamed with pride. But my mother bear instinct was still strong, as I still held a firm grip on the back of Eric's white, short sleeve polo shirt.

"Emma, honey you have to get down, you weigh too much for mommy to carry. Come on just stay in front of me and you'll be fine. Okay?"

However, if the situation wasn't bad enough already, the look on her face drew up feelings of dread as I knew what the look meant. "Excuse me agent, in about two seconds you're going to have another problem."

But my words barely got out, before I heard the sound of Emma throwing up. I couldn't fault her, because if I was her, I'd be throwing up, as a matter of fact, I didn't feel that great myself, but focusing on the obvious. I reached down and picked her up once again. "Honey, I don't know how much longer I can carry you, but I'll try okay." But she was scared beyond speech, and simply nodded before sticking her thumb in her mouth.

"Agent Montgomery, over here," an unknown dark-haired man in a bowler hat standing by the stairwell urged.

However, agent Montgomery also developed a look of fear. But hers didn't seem to be from the same threat we perceived to have, it appeared to be the man as she didn't seem to recognize him. This became clearer as she lined her weapon up with his chest from only four feet away and demanded his name and credentials. Although as he slowly reached into his pocket, his other hand that had been resting against his leg sprang up with lightning speed and sprayed a yellow missed in her face before she could react. Agent Montgomery fell to the ground, alerting us it was a nerve agent and to run.

I noticed the man seemed to be unphased by the noxious substance. This led me to believe, his immunity could only be brought on with experience with it. Now, running for our lives, I was afraid to stop and ask for any help as I no longer trusted anyone in sight. My mind raced with confusion through the chaos, but I managed to keep my attention or at least part of it on Eric and Emma. Somehow, we snaked our way through the halls and up to the service elevator but were met with a discouraging sign that said, 'out of service.'

"I just used that this morning, it's not out of service. Come on," Eric said, pulling the tape and sign away from the doors before hitting the UP button.

Chapter Five

The elevator took off with a jolt, running up the pole it was anchored to and made its way to the top floor, the doors slid open with a 'Ding' directly on the roof, next to a helicopter pad. But it was empty, and I thought we were screwed. Standing there, looking over the edge, a hushed chopping sound emanated from the other side of the building. Two hoverbikes piloted by special agents rose to meet us. Situating Emma in front of me, I instructed Eric to hold on tight to his pilot.

Raining like a banshee, the MIT designed vehicles sliced through the air like a hot knife through butter. Penetrating the clouds, we came dangerously close to the Tower of London. However, we veered off at the last moment giving us a closer look at Big Ben's backside, and landed in the meadow next to an old farmhouse that had a wisp of smoke dribbling from its chimney.

"Thank you," I said to her pilot while helping Emma off the seat. "Where do we go from here, I don't see anything."

But the pilot didn't respond verbally, instead gesturing to the farmhouse. However, Eric and his bike had landed yet, so not seeing it anywhere, I demanded her pilot tell me where he was, but again, he pointed to the small English style building and gunned his machines throttle. The aircraft resembling a motorcycle with 60-inch fan blades in the front and back lifted off the ground with a massive blast of wind and disappeared into the clouds.

"Where's Eric?" Emma asked, gripping my sweat-soaked hand.

"I'm not sure sweetheart," I said, wondering myself, but also taking solace in the fact that we all managed to get away safely.

The grass was wet under her feet, and longsword wrapped around her pant legs soaking them by the time we arrived at the heavily worn wooden door of the old building. Knocking, I cupped my hands around the fog riddled window next to a stack of old dried out corn stalks. But all I could see inside was a small cobblestone fireplace that was bursting with yellow and orange flames dancing around a half-burnt log.

Trying to get the homeowner's attention, Emma knocked this time, but after a few moments, we still hadn't received a response. Suddenly, the chilled breeze blew out of the South helping us make our decision to enter uninvited. Slowly, I turned the door handle, unlatching the metal strip that held it closed. Carefully, we walked through the small doorframe and made our way to the fireplace.

"Isn't this breaking and entering?" Emma asked, brushing her wet hair from her face.

"Well, technically we haven't broken anything, and the door was unlocked. So, if I had to guess it would be trespassing."

"I wondered how long it would take, for you to get here," a man's voice resonated from a dark area behind the chimney. The well-dressed Englishmen in the pinstripe suit stepped from the shadows. "My name is Belmont Wellington. I am the chief security officer of her Majesty's Secret Service. Welcome to England."

Swaggering over to the table, he poured himself a cup of tea and offered us one.

"Mr. Wellington, forgive my candor. But what the hell happened back there, I thought MI6 headquarters is supposed to be impenetrable?"

"Papa Bear knows you and your kids are here, and that love, makes them very nervous," Belmont said, sipping his tea but keeping his pinky up as is customary during afternoon tea.

"Why are they after us?" Emma asked, climbing up into a wooden chair next to the fireplace.

"Because my dear, you're the best of the best," Belmont replied, before raising his cup.

"What would they have done if they would've caught us?" I asked, almost afraid to get the answer.

"Well, not rightly sure, just don't get caught and you won't have to worry about it."

"Where's my son, we lifted off from MI6 at the same time, but he didn't land here, where is he?" I asked, trying to dry Emma's hair with a clean dish towel I found sitting on the counter next to the sink.

"He's fine, as a matter of fact," Belmont said, pulling a shiny gold pocket watch from his vest pocket attached by a gold chain. "Right about now, he should be on a plane to Australia."

"So, what do we do now, we can't just be here, speaking of which, where exactly are we?"

"A few miles outside of Liverpool, and no... you can't stay here this is a temporary safe house, it's not meant to keep people for any longer than a few hours. However, I did read in your file that you and your daughter are avid skiers. Is this correct, can you as they say hold your own?"

"I'm better than my mom, but I don't have my boots or skis. And what were those things we flew in on, how can I get one?" Emma asked, swatting my hand as I tried to dry the remaining strands of wet hair.

"Oh, I'm sorry they're not for public sale. Currently, they're only available to the military. Now if you both step over here, there are dry close and your weapons. Can I assume you were given instructions on how to operate them?"

"Yes," I said, handing Emma a thick wool sweater, and T-shirt. "Honey, take everything off and put it in a pile. Your soaking wet, I don't want you getting sick especially now of all times."

"Mom, is this jacket mine?" Emma asked, holding it up to admire the Commando Kidz logo embroidered on the front.

"Excuse me Mr. Belmont, are these jackets ours as well?"

"Yes, and as a matter-of-fact, your firstborn designed them. There's a built-in altimeter, that deploys a parachute if it senses a dramatic shift in your altitude and wind speed.

"That's fantastic," I said, examining the North face jacket that appeared to be nothing more than a regular down-filled jacket.

"It's bloody brilliant, is what it is. I know her Majesty's impressed. Now, you understand why the Russians find you and your children a threat?"

I nodded three times and slipped on the formfitting snug jacket. I slid my hand in the pocket and found a small surprise from Eric, a little Post-it note that said, "Love you, Mom." Which brought a tear to my eye, well it was either that or the random wisps of smoke that escaped the fireplace.

I figured Belmont was getting ready to make way as he reached for his hat hanging on a small coat rack that was fashioned out of deer antlers by the door. Pulling on his overcoat, and adjusting his hat, he turned and nodded. "Are you coming?" he asked, placing his hand on the front door.

"I guess we are, Emma zip up your coat. Where exactly are we going, Mr. Belmont?"

Our only contact with the outside world strolled with his cane as if he was on a Sunday afternoon walk toward a 60-inch wide polished aluminum snake then disappeared into the valley. I recognized it as the English and French pipeline that ran between the two countries and ended at the base of the Swiss Alps.

Through the fog, I could see the rest of the line stretching through the wavering buttercups that protruded through the English soil in the late afternoon breeze. The fragrance of lavender filled our noses as we shadowed Mr. Wellington. Eventually, he came to a stop, next to a section of the pipeline that appeared to be partially disassembled.

"What are we doing over here?" I said, crouching down to look at the underside of the engineering marvel.

"First, let me ask are you or the lass claustrophobic, you know you get in a tight spot and freak out?" he asked, waving his hands above his head.

"No," I said, shaking my head, looking down at Emma. Adding, "Do I dare even ask why?" and placing my hand on the door of the open section.

"Well, you've got the right idea, the best way to get you through is right under the noses. Now, certain times of the day, they send a test capsule through to push through any blockage that might obstruct the flow. The tubes avoided being flushed, but we fitted the capsule with a pair of oxygen masks."

"Wait... You want us to get inside there, look I appreciate all of your help Mr. Wellington, but there is no way in hell I'm sticking my daughter in a natural gas pipeline."

"Very well, you can take your chances here, just bear in mind love, if they found you back there, what's stopping them from finding you here, think about that one."

"But I don't understand," I said, "if we scare them, why are they chasing us?"

"Oh, well that's easy because they know you know where the map is, and they wanted."

"Wait... Pump the brakes Benny Hill, what map, nobody said anything about a map."

"Oh, did that slip their mind. All right, well in a nutshell you have to find..." he said, taking a long pause, "Hitler's hidden gold train."

"Are you joking, that's a myth, I watch a special on National Geographic about it Mr. Wellington. It doesn't exist, people have been looking for it since 1951 but nobody has ever recovered anything."

"Well, that's not entirely true... In 1944, Germany knew the end was near, so they took all valuables they had pillaged from Poland, France, and other countries and put them on a train. Some people said it headed for Belgium, others swear it ended up in Poland. That's why we need your help to find it. If Papa bear finds it before we do, you can be bloody sure the rightful owners of its contents will never see them again."

"So, in a nutshell, we're treasure hunters? I guess I'm okay with that, I'm not thrilled about everything else but...What do you think Emma, you want to find some buried treasure?"

"What's a gold train, and who is Hitler? Oh wait, isn't he that crazy German guy with a mustache that looks like mud under his nose?"

"Since World War II ended in 1945, the eerie story of the Nazi Gold Train has been passed down in Poland. While its authenticity has been contested over the years, it remained a central point of interest among the Polish people, who all know the story of the precious Nazi train car tucked away in the Owl Mountain tunnels."

Some Nazis took it upon themselves after the horrific events of the second World War to store artifacts in locations across Europe to prevent the army, ordinary people, and even fellow Nazis from having their hands on it. Many of those drop points were found in Eastern Europe in houses, castles, and Nazi-occupied areas. Nevertheless, it is believed that even more loot — especially the one stolen from detained/executed Jewish citizens — was hidden in Poland underground.

A labyrinth of hidden paths exists underneath the oldest mountain range in Poland, the Owl Mountains. What happened to those catacombs? From 1943 to 1945, Adolf Hitler, who admitted that the war did not go in favor of the Third Reich, ordered the construction of underground tunnels by Allied P.O.W.s so that they could be occupied and used by Nazi forces.

"Why do you think we can find it if all of your militaries can't, that doesn't make any sense Mr. Wellington?" Emma said, lightly stomping her freshly acquired boot in a puddle.

"We don't have much of a choice, we have been searching for this since basically the end of World War II. At one point, we thought we'd located it, but it was just another series of empty tunnels. So, we know the tunnels are there we just can't find the one that contains the train and its cargo."

"My daughter's right Mr. Wellington, I think you're setting yourself up for failure. Now, I'm not saying we can't find it, but I do think you should reconsider this fable of a train full of gold," I said, trying to reason with the man as daylight slipped away.

"Effectively, scholars haven't plotted out all other portions of the passages, and will never get the chance due to safety restrictions. But more curious explorers, history buffs, and Polish people have become fascinated with tunnel contents, with many thinking there's more to discover than the remains of war. Hitler's thousand-year Reich had collapsed in flames by the spring of 1945. The Allied armies which landed nearly a year earlier in Normandy had penetrated deep within Germany. The city was being shelled by Soviet troops, and by April Adolf Hitler, trapped in his fortress bunker, would commit suicide."

"That's all fine and good Mr. Wellington, but you still have it explained why you have such hope we can locate this that the experts haven't been able to, besides, why hasn't the Polish government stepped in and offered its assistance? Don't you think they would like to know if it is real and happens to be buried in their country?"

"Please understand, that would be a political nightmare. One we would like to avoid at all costs, of course, there would be a reward."

"Well, I am a single mother of two children, what kind of reward are we talking?"

"Rumor has it the train has 13 cars. Each contains 200 metric tons of gold, silver, and diamonds. Except for one, it supposedly has great works of art pillaged from Paris, the Netherlands, and Poland. The art alone is considered priceless, but if a number had to be placed on the contents of the entire train in today's money it would be two billion euros or around US$2.3 billion. In the reward specifications, I believe it's 10%."

"Oh, my God, that's $230 million, is my math right," I said, struggling to breathe.

"Bob's your uncle, so do we have a deal."

"Wait a minute, you haven't told us where we find the map?"

"You have to find a series of clues, and if you follow them diligently you should locate it. That's why we enlisted your son, because of his topography expertise. The area around Owl Mountain has changed dramatically over the past 70 years. However, Eric has shown extraordinary skill, determining the features of the landscape old and new. And this is why, we hope, from aerial reconnaissance photos from World War II as well as other documents we've acquired from that timeframe will give us a little more insight into where we should look. Because so far, it feels like we're looking for a needle in a haystack as they say."

I stopped for a moment to enjoy the beautiful scenery. That's why I wanted to take so many long walks along the breath-taking scenery back home, pushing stress out of my mind with the lush forests that I'd walk through, driving stress away.

As I stood looking around, Mr. Wellington answered Emma's questions. It was dead silent, except for the constant squawking of birds that produced beautiful rhythmic patterns that scattered through the rolling green hills. It relaxed my restless mind and killed all thoughts about our next mission.

Black cows with white spots chewed the tip of the wide blade grass, lazily grasping it as if they had all the time in the world. The sky was covered with a blueberry tint as the lemon-yellow sun began to disappear behind the mighty clouds. The fields were just massive. From this far away, they looked like perfect oblong formations with emerald green and royal blue hue that raised it to its brilliance.

<h1 style="text-align:center">Chapter Six</h1>

The dense dogwood trees enclosed the vast area of the countryside into the rugged terrain. The sky took on a gray tone much like a painter's painting. A farmer in the distance gathered his cows as they marched and ran through the overgrown property.

"I don't know how to ask this, but what would we do if we get caught? Is it like an embassy they take us to, or is it like a prisoner exchange?"

"I'm sorry, but that's not the way they work. Inside your backpack, you'll find a gold pen. It's in case the unthinkable happens. It's simple to operate, just place the tip to your skin and press the button. It's quick and painless."

"Mom, what does he mean 'quick and painless,' what's he referring top?" Emma asked, her eyes growing large because even though she was young, she had a vague understanding of what we were discussing.

"Nothing, he was just explaining if I needed a pen, that's all. Okay, Mr. Wellington, I believe we got rid of all the pleasantries. Let's get the show on the road, we're losing daylight."

"Very well, as I mentioned, this pipeline goes right through England. Now when it stops, if all goes as planned, you'll be in Paris. Now, there is a built-in GPS location system inside. So, we will track your location every inch of the way. There is a two-way transmitter in your headsets and emergency stop button on the console," he explained, pointing out every option.

"What about a bathroom, I have to pee?" Emma said, crossing her legs, and hopping around on one foot.

"Well, I don't mean to sound crude. But you have to go in the woods," Mr. Wellington, said gesturing to the tree line.

"Why can't she use the bathroom in the cottage?"

"Because there isn't one, did you not hear me say it's a temporary safe house? It's the size of a crumpet box, where would we put loo?"

"What's a loo?" Emily asked, starting to giggle.

"It's what you Americans call a toilet, but we find the term a bit randy."

"What's randy mean? Gross or icky?"

"Yes, spot on. It means icky, can we move along, please. It's my anniversary today, and I'd like to get home to the Mrs. before the stroke of midnight," Mr. Wellington announced, tipping the brim of his hat and placing a ladder over the cylindrical tube that still sparkled in the fading sunlight.

After Emma and I took a pee break, we hastily made our way back to Mr. Wellington.

"Okay honey, are you ready? You're not scared, are you?" I asked, but of course, my daughter had nerves of steel versus mine that were non-existent. I had lost those after the breach at Westminster Abbey.

"Righto, up you go," Mr. Wellington said, lifting Emma into the back chair of the eight-foot long tube and securing her into the three-point harness.

Stepping down the ladder, he gave me brief instructions on what to expect when we arrived in France. And how there would be another pair of agents from her Majesty's Secret Service waiting for us on the other side.

"If by the off chance, you feel queasy. There are excrement bags located under each of your seats. You mustn't get the control panel wet. If you short out the transmitter, or the translocation module we won't be able to track your movement and you'll be on your own. Understand," he said before closing the hatch over our heads.

Suddenly, the console lit up. Blue red and green lights filled the cabin, as our ears popped. From what I can only assume was caused by re-pressurizing the pipeline. Bizarrely, at first, we didn't know we were moving. But as we took the first dip down the hill, it was clear we were picking up speed.

I'm not claustrophobic, per se, but I'm not a fan of tight spaces either. But I figured, if it had to be done, we should be the ones to do it. When I was a little girl, my friends and I used to play on the beach, and pretended we found buried pirate treasure. We'd sit around drinking lemonade, and talk about what we would do if we ever found our imaginary booty.

The speed was clearly picking up, and since I didn't know the conversion rate between kilometers and miles, I could only guess we were going 200 miles an hour. The G forces building up on my chest, seemed to confirm it.

"How you doing honey, you hanging in there?" I asked, worrying about Emma's weak stomach.

"Un-huh... How much longer?" Emma asked, her voice trembling from the vibrations as the cylindrical container sped across the English countryside like a prized racehorse let loose from his stall.

The vibrations were growing stronger, alerting me that our speed had picked up. By now I figured we were doing close to 300 miles an hour by what the kilometer gauge was showing.

The terrain went on forever, off the Rolling Meadows, and down the hillsides. Even at one point going underwater, crossing the English Channel. The twists and turns were making me nauseous as I knew they were Emma. But my brain kept telling me to hold on, it wouldn't be much longer. However, during all of the excitement and chaos, I failed to ask our gracious English on loan from the Queen how long it would take to arrive in Paris. But my watch stopped working on the plane, so looking at it would be useless, although since I had time to kill I did anyway.

Of course, the hands hadn't moved since finding their final resting place at 11:02. Every dip or turn in the terrain made me nauseous, so I could only imagine how Emma was feeling. But I had to stay focused because all of this was so far out of my wheelhouse, it wasn't even funny. Yet I couldn't show it, knowing it would shake Emma's confidence and we all needed as much as we could get, so I swallowed my fear back and toughened up.

But as I was giving myself a pep talk in my head, I could feel the capsule slowing. Not sure if I should be happy or scared, I kept my thoughts to myself, hoping Emma wouldn't notice. However, sometimes I forget how inquisitive she is, within just a few seconds of me noticing, her voice echoed through the headset, "Mom? I think we're slowing down, and I'm not a whiz at geography, but I don't think were in France yet."

"I know, I was thinking the same thing. Can you reach your backpack?" I asked, maneuvering my arms to where I could reach my own.

I think so," Emma said, also shifting her torso to reach her satchel.

"Get your 'STOP' gun out. Because I've got a bad feeling, we may need them."

After a couple of minutes of silence, Emma announced, "Okay, mine's locked and loaded," followed by the sound of the device powering up.

"Hey honey, how...?"

"Push the green button on the handle, then wait for the digital readout near the trigger to flash 'charged,' it takes about 10 seconds. Do you see it, did it work?"

Examining my nonlethal weapon, I did as my daughter instructed, and within the 10-second timeframe, the word 'Charged' flashed repeatedly in the housing of the timer.

Which I could only assume, means the weapon's ready. I just didn't know if we were because as a laid my weapon in my lap, my hand shook. Even though I was trying to be strong, it was still difficult, I'd never been in the situation before of course, in a pinch I can always rely on my daughter since she appeared to have more experience dealing with this type of thing that I did. Which even thinking, was ludicrous, at least up until recently anyway. Abruptly, the capsule came to a halt, I carefully pushed one of my headset headphones away from my ear as I thought I heard voices. However, they didn't sound English or American. It almost appeared they were speaking German, but I couldn't be sure at least not as of yet.

Suddenly, Emma's voice broke the silence, "Mom? Why did we stop, what's going? I hear voices outside, their speaking German."

"Yeah, that's what I thought too, can you tell what they're saying?"

"Hurry, hurry get them out. There is no time to waste, move, move!"

Hearing this, my stomach tightened, and beads of perspiration formed on my temple. I clenched my hand around my weapon, keeping my hand on the trigger. Dripping on the plexiglass that covered the top of the capsule, was molten like substance, closely resembling lava. It was coming from a torch, a welding torch that was being used to cut into the pipeline. However, I still wasn't convinced we were in France yet, and this concerned me greatly. So, I don't know if it was my paranoia, or just being overzealous, but I instructed Emma to shoot first and ask questions later.

"Honey, you shoot the first person you see. Understand?" Not being able to see, if she acknowledged my instructions, I ask again.

Although this time she responded, "Okay, I will, love you, Mom. Also, I want to tell you, I don't blame you for the divorce."

"Thank you, honey, that means a lot but maybe right now we should pay attention to what's happening here. We'll worry about that stuff later, okay. But thank you," I said, my eyes welling up with tears.

Beaming through the capsule with a sliver of daylight, the scarce sunlight illuminated the area around us, eventually exposing two men and a woman, one holding the torch still burning a bright blue flame. They spoke in German, but before I could ask Emma what they were saying, they pulled the canopy back. So, of course, I yelled, "FIRE," causing my pint-size mini-me to unload her weapon into two of the men.

"Nice shot honey."

Standing up in the capsule, we could see both men rolling on the ground, eventually becoming motionless but still able to blink showing they were still conscious. The woman, donning a beret and a red vest quickly raised her hands and spoke in broken English, "Halt firing, we are friendly. We assure your safe travels; we mean you no harm."

"Where are we, this doesn't look like France," I said, pointing my weapon at the unknown German accomplice.

I was afraid to relax, so I didn't lower my weapon at first, I still had too many questions. Glancing around at my surroundings, I could see the rolling hills in the small pocket of sheep just off to her left, again giving me confidence, we were still in England. But I didn't see anyone else, just the two men on the ground and the Fraulein my weapon was trained on which I found strange. If they were so worried about us, why would they only send three, because I remember at Westminster Abbey there were at least 50.

"Why did you stop us, and why are we not in England?" Although at first, she appeared hesitant to speak, thinking it could be my gun, I slowly lowered the barrel from her face to her chest. "You better start talking because I've had one hell of a day. And I don't have the patience for the likes of you."

"We received instructions from MI6 that the Russians discovered their plan to use the pipeline," the German resident said, lowering her hands. "We were told to get you out before checkpoint N93, it's where the line splits off to the right, you would go to Belgium to the left you would end up in France. We shouldn't be standing here, we are just targets if we do," she said, checking on her compatriots.

"They'll be okay in a few hours. Probably," Emma said, stepping on the aluminum frame of the capsule. Holding her hand out, our unexpected rescuer assisted her as she climbed down a small ladder that had been placed next to the pipeline.

Eventually, our feet were back on firm ground, we discussed our next plan of attack. It was relatively clear, this was not going to be a walk in the park, because it seemed everyone and their mother knew we were there and every one of them wanted a piece of us. Not a fun thought, knowing someone wants to hurt your children, but oddly I felt more scared for the bad guys when they encountered them, because I knew Emma, was a sure shot with lightning speed and had graduated at the top of her martial arts class. And I knew Eric was the smartest person I'd ever met. So, I figured if they really needed somebody to save the world, they came to the right people.

Scanning the area, I couldn't help but notice the snow that appeared to be fresh fallen covering the landscape. "How do you have snow here, already?" "It's a tad colder here than Liverpool. We are just a hop skip and a jump from Paris, the climate there varies. Although currently, we're just starting winter."

Off in the distance, a low whining rumble could be heard. They were the exhaust coming from snowmobiles. Shaking the ground as they approached, one of them clipped the branches of a 30-foot birch tree causing the snow that had accumulated throughout the days' storm system to fall to the ground. Pulling up beside us, just be the way, one of the drivers instructed Emma to get on with him and me to get on one of the other three that had pulled up.

Our drivers handed us a pair of goggles. Within just a few seconds of adjusting them snugly around our eyes, we were whisked away in the diminished daylight. We drove for hours, up and over the hills and through the woods, following trails that had been used for years. The vibration of the machine against my legs made my knees itch and the exhaust made me feel nauseous on occasion. Eventually, we came up to a deep valley and without warning, headed towards it. As the blinding snow parted ways, I could see a small cottage with four silhouettes standing beside it.

The 600cc high-performance British government issued snowmobiles came to a halt, inches from which I could can see were people. Yet, they didn't appear to be fearful and didn't move. Instead, they rushed over to help us off machines and then hurried us inside the quaint structure.

"Good evening," the first man said, in a French accent. He was ruggedly handsome, with a 5 o'clock shadow. "I'm sure, you wonder why you are here, yes?"

I nodded, three times, but was still trying to warm my hands next to the fireplace that was roaring bright in the first room we had entered.

"When MI6 suffered a breach back in England. They determined it was because of infiltration, double agents. People who were working both sides of the grid, so, unfortunately, the people you thought you could trust, you can't," he finished, sipping what I could only assume was tea."

"I'm hungry, I need something to eat," Emma said, taking off her gloves and putting them in her pocket.

"Of course, where are my manners. I make a very nice crêpe with pork and brie."

"What's a crêpe, and what's brie. We have a girl at our school named Paris, she's a mean little b I t c h."

"Emma! Language!" I knew she's under stress, but I couldn't handle my children using vulgar language. As I'd taught them to use their brains and not their mouths but kids will be kids.

The enticing aroma that was coming from the cast-iron skillet was heavenly. As he sautéed the thinly sliced strips of ham, he poured in a dab of olive oil, before adding some scallions and a handful of wild mushrooms he had picked out from the local farmers market earlier in the week.

Chapter Seven

Putting the delicately cooked ingredients in a small bowl off to his right, he grabbed another one that was filled with whipped egg and poured it in the pan. Allowing it to cook for only a couple of minutes, he quickly grabbed the cooked ingredients and placed them back in the pan, but this time inside the pillowy egg pancake. Adjusting the ingredients, he carefully flipped over one side of the egg and then the other until it made a nice cocoon.

Looking on, my mouth watered as we both hadn't eaten for a few hours and my stomach had been grumbling from the time we entered the capsule back in England. Our host noticed me gazing at the gourmet concoction asked, "I have enough for one more, can you eat, are you...hungry, madam?"

"I guess I could eat," I said, attempting to hide my growing hunger pains.

"Please, have a seat. So, tell me, how has your trip been to Europe so far?" he said introducing himself is Sean Phillippe.

"Well, the flight over was interesting," I said, shoveling another forkful of the steaming food into my waiting mouth.

"How so, was she bumpy?" he asked, in a thick but debonair French accent.

"Yeah, you could say that both of our pilots got sucked out. So, we had to land the plane."

The normally subtle Frenchman choked on his food for a moment. "Your... Pilots? Gone?"

"Oh yeah, I mean they didn't die. But something hit the windshield, and suck both of them out, it was only by the grace of God they got caught on shards of glass and held in place until we landed," I said, my taste buds hurting as I savored the delectable food.

"You must be kidding, that is miraculous? So, how long have you been a spy?"

"On and off 10 years, but her and my son just two years. How long have you been doing this?"

"Many, many years. My father, he too was a spy. Just like his father, and his father before him. I guess you could say, it's part of our family tree."

"That's amazing, and so is this food. I've never had anything like this, are you a chef part-time."

Taking off his hat, he ran his fingers through his auburn brown hair which made his deep blue eyes sparkle. "No. All French people can cook, it's a law."

"Really? I did not know that, I guess I learned something new today," I said, naïvely accepting his reply.

"I am just how you say. Bluffing you? My mother was a very good cook. When I was a boy on Sundays when our family gathered, she would show me things, so it is an inherited skill."

Suddenly, the sound of rapid gunfire broke the darkness that covered the vast expanse. Multiple voices could be heard from just outside the cottage door, causing Sean Phillippe to drop his fork on the ridge of his plate and lookup. A couple of minutes pass before he stood up and announced, "Come. They have found you. Hurry, follow me," he said, leading us out the back of the cottage to an idling snowmobile.

"What's happening? How did they find us, so fast?" I said, grabbing Emma's hand.

"I don't know, but you don't have time to waste. Your driver, he will stop at nothing to get you to the next checkpoint, so do as he says. Good luck to you both, and Godspeed," he said, patting Emma on her blue ski-hat.

Abruptly, the snow on both sides of the snowmobile began exploding, erupting into six-inch clouds of snow as the bullets ricocheted around us. Our driver gave the machine full throttle, causing it to lurch up and grab the snow, shooting us away from the structure like a random bolt of lightning leaving the cloud. Although this ride was a bit bumpier than the last, we had taken on the machines.

Skimming the snow, the snowmobile's headlight pierced the night, illuminating the rolling hills covered with untouched snow. Occasionally, we could hear the winding of the engine over the noise the 18-inch tracks made as it gripped the ground beneath it. The evening air was chilled, but not ice-cold as I predicted it would be as we plowed through it. Although cold enough to make our teeth chatter uncontrollably.

Wondering if we would ever reach our destination, the gasoline-powered sled began to slow as it crept along a ridgeline next to the base of the mountain.

"Why did we stop? I don't see anything," I said, right before the flood of lights began beaming from every direction. I could make out five cars and three trucks through the eye-watering headlights. I instructed Emma, as before "shoot first, ask questions later."

But after remaining on the snowmobile like sitting ducks for what seemed like an eternity, I threw my leg off the back to take a closer look around and tried to determine if they were friend or foe. "Can you cut, the high beams, please?"

"Ms. Elkin," I heard, emanating from one of the cars.

"Who's asking?" I snapped, in no mood for the constant theatrics.

A tall man wearing an overcoat and earmuffs stepped away from his car. "Agent Nichols, Central Intelligence Agency," he announced.

"Oh, thank God, an American. What the hell is going on agent?" I asked in an unusually demanding tone.

"It seems you're in high demand, I can't remember the last time we had spies tracked as heavily as you three."

"Thank you, I think? How are we ever supposed to find this, quote-unquote map if it even really exists if we keep getting shot at?" I said, knocking the snow away from my boots.

"We were getting shot at? I didn't know that. How come nobody told me?" Emma said, in a tiny voice.

"Oh, the map is real, I can assure you of that, it's just a matter of finding it. Now, we were sent here to give you a buffer, and hold off the Ruskies," agent Nichols said, leading us back behind his vehicle.

Sitting on the ground, and covered with a camouflaged tarp, I could see the back end of a seat of a hoverbike.

Agent Nichols, grabbed the corner of the tarp and yanked it back, causing the freshly fallen snow covering it, to billow up like a cloud. Emma realizing it was a hoverbike, squealed with excitement, however, I did not share her enthusiasm. Simply because I wasn't in a good driver behind the wheel of a car, let alone a motorcycle that flew.

I tried to relax, and listen to agent Nichols's instructions. But I couldn't get by the fear, so his words were muffled and indistinguishable. I felt my knees shaking, and the paranoia creeping through my body like a rampant fever. But Emma's excitement, kind of squashed that because I figured if a child should enjoy this, maybe I shouldn't be so scared.

"Okay, hop on now. Remember, the left handle has this blue button," he said pointing his penlight flashlight at it that he had dug out of his shirt pocket, "if you push up, you go up. If you push it down, you're going to go down. So, make sure wherever it is you go down, is unobstructed and not in the water, they do not have any buoyancy. That means they don't float. Now, on the right handle, you have a throttle, obviously, this will increase your speed."

"This is going to be so cool, can I drive," Emma remarked with a giggle, hopping up on the machine before agent Nichols finished giving his instructions.

"Here, these helmets are fitted with transponders and two-way radios. They'll help you communicate with each other but also with your contacts once you get closer to Paris."

"How do we know if we're going in the right direction agent? I'm not great with directions," I said, straddling the large machine.

"Don't worry about that, it's pre-programmed into its computer. You couldn't get lost if you tried. All you have to worry about is staying high enough so you don't clip any buildings or trees. Let the bike do all the work, all right."

"How do we start it?" I asked, my hands trembling on the handlebars.

"Just push the up button, and then give her some gas she'll do the rest," agent Nichols said, patting the windshield of the machine.

As soon as my thumb touched the blue button, there was a "Whooshing," first in the front and then the back. Before I knew it, I could see the ground getting further away as we rose into the night sky only illuminated by a half of the moon. Carefully, I twisted back the rubber-coated handle. At first, the pace was slow and fairly staggered. But as I got more comfortable, I gave it more gas until finally, I couldn't turn it back anymore. Looking down at the gauges, it said we were going a hundred miles an hour, but because of the windshield, it didn't feel like it.

The craft silently skipped through the night sky like a stone over a pond. Emma's tiny gloves wrapped around my waist as she rested her head on my back. But fearing she would fall off, I couldn't allow her that luxury. And told her so through the headset before directing my attention to what was in front of us. A seemingly endless sky, with few stars, showing.

Feeling the winter air on our faces, I looked at the console and could see we still had a way to go. However, while examining it, I noticed an autopilot button. Fearing the worst at first, I didn't push it. As agent Nichols hadn't described what it did, harboring on the up and down and throttle buttons only.

However, I feared if I didn't, I would fall asleep and tumble off, which I knew would certainly sentence Emma to an untimely death. After debating the issue for a couple of minutes, I knew I didn't have a choice. So, I pushed it.

But after a second or two, I couldn't see any change in the vehicle's performance. Although just as I was losing hope, thinking it hadn't engaged, I noticed a small green light on the dashboard, and after squinting at it I could tell the autopilot was engaged. Relaxing my shoulders, I let the seatbelt hold me into place as I gripped Emma's hands which were firmly around my waist and rested my head on the dashboard right below the windshield.

I dreamt about Eric, hoping he was all right. But even in my dream, I assured myself he would be, simply because of his intellect and training. I found myself walking down a cobblestone path to where I approached a rod iron gate that was rusty on the bottom and had black paint peeling on the top of it.

There was an old colonial-style mansion, with broken windows in the open front door behind it. I remember I had seen the house before; I just couldn't place it. Pushing open the gate, I stepped across the threshold and looked at the house. There was something about it that made the hair on my neck stand up, but I didn't want to venture any further fearing I would find out what. So, I took a step back, and as I did the gate slammed shut almost catching my fingers in it.

Quickly, I pulled myself awake, telling myself it was just a dream. But it took me a couple of moments to regain my bearings and remember where I was, of course, it didn't take long due to the cool breeze slamming against my face like pebbles from a slingshot.

The sun was rising just off in the distance, filling the sky with orange and yellow hues. It resembled a tangerine smoothie. I gently shook Emma's hands.

"What? I don't want to go to school today, I don't feel good," she responded.

"Oh my God, Emma? Look, it's the Eiffel Tower. It's beautiful, I've never seen it this close all lit up."

"Wow, it is spectacular. I've always wanted to go on it, do you think we'll have time?" she asked, looking over my shoulder.

"I'm not sure, but you know that the Eiffel Tower had reddish-brown paint when it opened in 1889. Then, ten years later, it was painted yellow? You know, every seven years, painters add 60 tons of paint to keep the tower young and bright. It is painted in three shades, increasingly lighter with elevation to increase the profile of the structure against the canvas of the Parisian sky."

"Why did they build it? Is it like the Statue of Liberty, I learned in school that France sent us that too."?

"Well, the organizing committee of the 1889 fair, which commemorated the 100th anniversary of the fall of Bastille and the start of the French revolution, staged and opened the competition to design a magnificent flagship for their world fair. Out of the 107 proposals, designs submitted by architect Stephen Sauvestre and engineers Maurice Koechlin and Emile Nouguier were chosen."

"It's so big, why is it so tall mom? Did they want everyone to see it?" Emma asked, staring intently at the French architectural marvel.

"It was the highest structure in the world for four decades. At 986 feet, the Eiffel Tower was almost twice the height of the previous Washington Monument structure when it opened in 1889. It would not be exceeded until the construction of the 1,046-foot Chrysler building in New York in 1930, although the Eiffel Tower passes the height of the Chrysler building with the introduction of the 1957 radio antenna, it is still trailed behind another skyscraper, the Empire State Building in New York City."

"Isn't the guy Eiffel, the same one who built our Statue of Liberty, too?"

"Yes. Ironically, when the original builder of the Statue of Liberty's interior components died unexpectedly in 1879, French sculptor Frederic-Auguste Bartholdi appointed Eiffel as his successor. Eiffel, already renowned as a structural engineer and railway bridge builder, designed the steel support structure to which the copper skin of the statue is attached. Today, a scale model of the Statue of Liberty stands on an island in the Seine River in the shadow of the Eiffel Tower."

"That's incredible, I didn't know that, is it also true it helped win World War I?"

"In a way, throughout World War I, the French army used a wireless tower transmitter to receive German messages from Berlin. In 1914, the French became able to plan a counter-offensive, mostly during the Battle of the Marne, after unexpectedly discovering that the German forces were preventing its advancement. Three years later, the antenna at the top of the Eiffel Tower intercepted a secret signal between Germany and Spain that provided information of "Operative H-21." Partially, based on this communication, the French captured, convicted, and executed legendary spy Mata Hari for espionage on behalf of Germany."

"Wow! I didn't know that either. Hey, Mom have you noticed these jackets are a little heavier than our other ones?" Emma announced, taking her right hand off my waist as she tried to maneuver her arm in and out of the sleeve.

"Are you nuts? Put your hand back, right now!" I snapped, attempting to make her aware of her situation.

It was useless, of course, because I couldn't blame her, if it wasn't for the life-threatening danger around every corner, I would be having a good time too. But as it stood, so far, I had had to land a jumbo jet, been shot at, had nerve gas thrown in my face, zipped down a natural gas pipeline, traversed the English countryside in the dead of night, and was currently driving a flying motorcycle. Of course, the thing that scared me about all of this was it all happened in less than two days.

Finding its way from behind the clouds, the Parisian sun climbed into the sky at a turtle's pace. Yet still having enough work to bask over our faces and exposed appendages. My nose was beginning to run, and with the cold air in constant play, it was hard to be avoided. So, I tried to hide it when I used my jacket sleeve to wipe my nose. Although my astute daughter, quickly picked up on it.

"I thought you said my sleeve isn't a Kleenex, doesn't that mean yours isn't either?"

Chapter Eight

"I did, and it's not, except for situations like this, is your face numb too, or is it just me?"

"No, it's not just you. I haven't been able to feel my nose and cheeks for the last hour. Are we almost there yet, how much longer?" Emma asked, adjusting herself on the seat and causing the bike to tilt slightly before automatically leveling itself again.

"It shouldn't be much longer," I said, shaking my head to emphasize, "the little dot, shows we should be right over our target. I hope pressing the autopilot button, didn't mess things up."

As the machine heard my concern, it began to slow its forward momentum. Stopping momentarily to hover in a stationary manner. A white light illuminated on the dashboard, next to a small icon that appeared to be an arrow pointing down, but I wasn't completely sure as my eyes hadn't stopped watering yet.

Descending slowly, I could just make out three figures standing directly below us, as did Emma. "Aren't they gonna move? Beep the horn Mom."

"Sweetheart, you do know that we're supposed to be stealth, you know secretive? We don't want to attract unwanted attention, okay. Plus, I don't know if this thing even has a horn, frankly, I'm afraid to push anything."

"Agent Nichols gave us instructions, didn't you pay attention?"

"Yes. But I kinda have other things on my mind, like oh I don't know, keeping us alive."

"When I don't pay attention, I get grounded. How come you don't get grounded?"

"Okay, fair enough when we get back you can ground me. So, how much time am I going to get warden?"

"Thirty-one years!" Emma said, giggling.

After two or three minutes, the craft came to rest, right beside the North leg of the Eiffel tower. The structure was breath-taking, almost too much for the eyes to bear as it rose into the clouds. The white brilliant lights tastefully draped over her exoskeleton, made her resemble a metal Angel glimmering in the morning sun.

"Bonjour mademoiselle, quel est votre nom?"

"I'm sorry, I don't speak French, Emma can you translate?"

"Oh, I beg your pardon. Hello Miss, what is your name?"

I hesitated to answer because I was instructed not to trust anyone. But after giving them a once over, I felt I didn't have much of a choice, after all I did just land a non-licensed aircraft feet from the base of the Eiffel tower. Which I knew had to be illegal for some reason or another, so I answered. "My name is Brenda Elkin; this is my daughter Emma. We work for the United States Central intelligence agency or you may know it as the CIA."

"Very well, it's nice to meet you, my name is Françoise, and these are my colleagues Donatello, and Capriccio. We are here to assist you, you may leave your machine here, as it will be transported back to England. Follow me, if you please."

"Wait a minute, you can't expect us just to walk off with you willy-nilly. How do we know, you're not one of them, you know a counterspy?"

Françoise puckered his lips. "I guess you don't understand, the longer we stand here the better the chance of you being discovered. So, please, may we go now?"

I nodded simultaneously with Emma as we were both fixated on the Frenchman's face. His accent was so strong, we had to read his lips. But after a few moments we got the gist of the point he was attempting to make and shadowed his every step.

We were led over to a patch of skinny evergreen trees. He took a lingering look around, getting a 360° view before turning his attention back to the trees. Suddenly, he slipped in between them but didn't come out the other side. Poking his hand through, he gestured us to follow, and we did, first Emma them myself. To our surprise in between the dense foliage, was a staircase, a winding rod iron one that traveled underground at least 100 feet.

Getting down to what appeared to be the ground-level, I glanced above our heads to see a metal shield close off the entrance. We walked down a narrow hallway that was decorated with pictures from World War II. It was mostly pilots, and decorated soldiers with the exclusion of the picture of Winston Churchill that hung on the wall next to a door that was labeled 'war room.'

"May I get you something to drink, or something to eat. Are you hungry?" the middle-aged Frenchman with gray hair asked, gesturing with his hand to his mouth.

Wasting no time, Emma quickly replied, "I am, I'm starving."

"How about you, can I make you something? We have a fully staffed kitchen and some of the finest ingredients in the world. Just name your delicacy."

"I would really like some ham and eggs, and a couple of pieces of toast lightly buttered, is that doable?" I said, crossing my mental fingers.

"Wee, how about you small one?" he asked, taking Emma's order next.

"French toast! May I please have powdered sugar and cinnamon?"

"Of course, what would you like to drink, we have coffee, espresso, orange, and grapefruit juices?"

"Do you have any chocolate milk? I'll be your best friend for life," Emma asked, hanging on Françoise every word.

"I will see, what we can muster up. But I'm sure we can arrange something, how about you Madam?"

"I would love espresso; I know I can definitely use one or 10."

"Of course, I will bring you your first three and then tell me if you want more, have you experienced espresso before, she is very strong?" he asked, smiling wide.

"Oh, well, in that case just bring me one to start. If after that I don't get so wired, I have to run a marathon, I'll take another."

"Very well, sit back and relax. Our commander, Alisha Pannette will be in momentarily. She will be debriefing you, all right, I will be back."

I loosen the strings in my boots, as my feet were sweating profusely. Unzipping my jacket, I put it on the back of the chair and adjusted my shirtsleeves as they were pulling on my shoulders ever since we'd gotten on the hoverbike. I stood up to get a closer look at the pictures donning the walls of the tactfully decorated room.

"That picture there was taken December 1941. Two hours before the Germans blitzed England and France. Of course, after which most of both countries had to be rebuilt afterward. Good morning, my name is commander Alisha Pannette, of the French special forces. Welcome to Paris Ms. Elkin, and who might you be?" the woman in the blue uniform, decorated with multiple French metals asked Emma.

"My mother taught me, never to talk to strangers. And you're the strangest looking stranger I've ever seen."

Bizarrely though, out of the corner of my eye, I could see an odd look on my daughter's face. One I'd only seen once before through the living room window when the dog in our neighborhood got loose and stared her down in the middle of the street. She said later, she could tell there was something wrong with the way the dog walked, and she knew it was going to chase her. So, she didn't trust the commander any more than she trusted that dog. I needed to find out why.

So, I whispered in her ear, "What's wrong?" at the same time pretending to scold her as not to raise suspicion."

"I don't trust her, there's something strange about her Mom."

"Just follow my lead, don't go off half-cocked," I replied, whispering back in her ear.

"You know what, I left something on the bike. I'll just run up and get it, I'll be right back."

Emma and I got to our feet at the same time and began walking towards the entrance. However, the commander had a different idea and called our bluff. "You know, you'll never get out of here alive. Trying is futile, just take us to the map and we can see to it your demise is quick. You don't want your daughter to suffer because of your ignorance and failure to cooperate, now, do you?"

"The only one that's going to suffer commander, is you. LIGHT HER UP M!"

We must have been running on the same wavelength, because simultaneously Emma and I trained our 'STOP' guns on Alisha's chest and opened fired, striking her multiple times. Like the other two victims before her, she rolled on the ground in pain until after 30 seconds when she stiffened and got hard as a board.

"Mom! That was badass, wasn't it!"

"Yes, it sure was but please watch your language."

"Mom, Mr. Rogers uses harsher language than you do, lighten up."

Now, the fun really began, trying to get out of there. I remembered the hallways, and how we had to take a left turn and right to get in here. But I didn't remember the code that Françoise had pushed when he opened the first set of doors.

"What's wrong Mom, why did we stop?"

"I can't remember the code, I wasn't paying attention," I said, hovering over the keypad.

"I do, it's 77613," Emma announced, pushing the charge button, again.

Stunned by my daughter's memory, I entered the code into the pad quickly, which turned the light green, and flashed a sign stating access was granted. We climbed up the ladder with no time to waste, as agents were on our heels, I couldn't believe what was happening. But taking time for a reality check, wouldn't have been the best move as I remembered the gold pen I was given prior to the start of the mission.

After climbing at least 100 feet, we pushed open the round hatch that had closed over our heads earlier and stepped up onto the surface but noticed our hover vehicle was missing. Although I figured considering what could've happened, losing that was the least of our problems. However, looking around, I saw two men who seemed to be moving quicker than the usual leisurely pace I had noticed most French citizens took as they strolled through the scenery. As I looked to my right, I noticed two more also moving at a hurried pace.

Running out of places to go, Emma pointed to a sign, that was in French.

"It's an elevator, come on Mom this way," Emily yelled, pulling my hand in that direction.

However, its operator was a bit rattled, as we both had ran on out of breath, and were sweating because of our heavy gear.

"Tickets?"

At first, I didn't understand what he said, of course, Emma did and reached in her back pocket and to my surprise pulled out a $20 bill.

"Merci beaucoup, merci beaucoup pour votre accueil," the operator spouted pocketing the US currency.

"What did he say?" I asked, feeling foolish I didn't have a better grasp on their language.

"He just said 'thank you for your hospitality.' You really should brush up on your French, Mom. You are a teacher, after all."

"I'm sorry, piloting flying motorcycles picks up too much of my time," I said, rolling my eyes.

As I looked over my shoulder, I could see we had company, so I nudged the lift operator and pointed up. I'm not sure if he understood we were being chased or not, but I did find it rather interesting he told one of the men who approached the closed rod iron gate they would have to wait for the next car. But as we rose higher into the air, I could see our company wasn't restricted to the ground below.

Running up the stairs, trying to catch our car, two more men followed us until we reached the second observation deck.

Understanding the clandestine nature of our mission was pertinent, so was staying alive. So, I made an executive decision, "Emma, charge them up," because I knew our 'S.T.O.P.' weapons would do exactly that but this was another reason. I thought the elevator operator was on our side because even as she pulled the futuristic-looking device from her knapsack he didn't bat an eye. Instead, he just watched the men as they appeared to be multiplying, running up the stairs.

"Dernier étage. Nous ne pouvons pas aller plus loin," he said, opening the gate.

"What, hey M, a little translation please?"

"He said 'top floor, and we can't go any further.' Come on, I've got an idea."

"Hey, I'm in charge I'll give the orders! So, what do you think we should do now?"

"Mom, I never thought I'd ask you this, but do you know how to fight?"

"I've been a stay-at-home mother for the last seven years, what do you think?"

Unfortunately, I didn't have time to think as two men jumped down from the balcony right above our heads and dropped down in front of us. Suddenly, I heard Emma yell, "YAH, YAH!"

Kicking one of the men in the face, she dropped down and punched another man in the groin, immobilizing both of them. But another one ran from around the backside of the observation deck and had a pipe. Swinging wildly meticulously, Emma avoided each swing. Dropping back down into her stance, she jumped up and executed a perfect roundhouse kick across the man's chin. Knocking him off his feet, however, he had company, as three more ran up the steps to assist.

The sound of the nonlethal weapon filled the air, "WHOOSH, WHOOSH!" But there were still too many, there had to be 50 or more agents after us and there was nowhere to go as the lift operator had already returned to the ground floor. I yelled, "THERE"S TOO MANY!"

"MOM? FOLLOW ME," Emma said, heading for a door. It had a yellow arrow on it that pointed up. Running up the stairs, we could hear the men close behind us, yelling, "Arrêter, Arrêter!" Which I understood, it meant 'stop.'

As I turned the corner, I was exposed to a sight that no parent should ever witness, Emma was standing on the handrail 900 feet above the ground. I'm scared to say anything.

"EMMA! GET DOWN!"

"We've got no choice Mom. JUMP........" she said before diving off the railing. But my horror turned to elation as I saw her parachute pop from the back of her jacket, and arrested her fall, although strangely, it displayed a British flag instead of an American one.

With that said, I'd never been a big fan of heights because when I was a child, I fell out of a birch tree in the front yard and broke my arm.

Chapter Nine

Ever since then, gravity and I have never gotten along. But as I look behind me, two men had turned into 10 and they had guns. So outmanned and outgunned I had no choice, "I trust you, Eric," I said, climbing up on the handrail.

I pushed off just as one of the men's hand was going for my pant leg. At first, it felt like I hung there in the air until my chute opened up abruptly and snapped me back skyward. Emily was only 1000 feet or so in front of me. From a distance, she appeared to be riding the light in the sunrise as she floated aimlessly.

Noticing a pair of handles, one on each side of the chute I grabbed them. I remembered something I'd seen in a movie about how they controlled the direction and rate of descent. This apparently was something Emma already knew, as she was circling back around to my location.

I could hear her yell something, but she was too far away for me to make it out.

"ALL WE NEED IS SOME JAMES BOND MUSIC!" I made out as she circled around me again like she was riding an aerial-skateboard.

"Yep, my kids are insane," I said to myself but not diluting the fact we had survived.

Of course, now the remaining question was how we were supposed to get down. But just as I thought we were out of danger, there came a "BUZZZZZZZZ!" Now what? I thought.

Looking behind me, I could see a motorized paraglider quickly gaining on us. The roar of his engines pulled up beside of us, close enough for me to raise my weapon and fire my last round from my 'S.T.O.P.' gun. My projectile hit its target, stalling the aircraft's engine.

After turning the motorized parachute into nothing more than a glider that couldn't keep up with us, we pressed on.

"How long can we stay aloft?" I asked Emma over the howling breeze, still bitter from the morning cold.

"Depends on our airflow. As long as we can sustain lift, 10 maybe 15 minutes. I don't see them anymore, do you?" Emma said, wiping her nose with her sleeve. Her eyes were watering so bad from the continuous burst of air, I was surprised she could see.

"No. But that doesn't mean they're not down there," I said, looking over my shoulder and down between the harness and the ground, scanning the terrain for any unfriendlies that could still be scouting for us. Of course, they hadn't given up that easy because I saw three of them directly below us, pointing up and talking to a policeman.

But the cop didn't really seem to care, by now the breeze was beginning to die down. So, I knew our window of hovering escape would be coming to an end. I needed to figure out another way to keep us safe but also get us to our next drop point.

However, chagrin I heard the phone ring. The first thought was I was delirious. But then, I heard it again and observed it was a hidden pocket I hadn't noticed before. So, carefully, I unzipped the nylon-like material, and retrieved the device. The caller ID just read, 'INCOMING CALL,' but I figured I didn't have anything to lose
"Hello?" I answered.

"Well, this is a pleasant surprise. You're still alive, I'm impressed Ms. Elkin, you left with such haste, I didn't get a chance to explain where you would find your next clue. When you land, you're going to see a red farmhouse with two white cows. You will proceed inside, where inside a pot of water that is sitting on the stove, you will find a key. Along with this, you will find instructions on where to go next, but keep in mind Ms. Elkin, currently, you have half the KGB after you. I would use caution, extreme caution. This message will self-destruct in five seconds. 5-4-3-2-1."

"CRAP! The little suckers on fire," I said after I dropped it and watched it explode after hitting the ground.

"What was that all about?" Emma asked, eyeballing a field, just off in the horizon.

"It was a recorded message, telling me we'd see a red farmhouse and a couple of cows."

"Well, there is a farmhouse. I can't tell if it's right or not, it's still too far away. But those are definitely cows," she said, pointing to the bovines that dotted the small farm.

Needless to say, my landing was less than perfect. I landed butt first in a fresh pile of cow manure. Which of course gave Emma a good laugh. But the air was heavy with fog, as the morning sunlight had not burned it off yet. The grass crunched under our feet as we made our way to the front door of the dilapidated building.

Walking into the sparsely furnished structure, I kept my guard up. I didn't who to trust. But I remembered what the message described and where it said to find our next clue. So logically that was all that was important, well that and staying alive. However, that was getting more and more challenging by the minute. Especially now, after learning Soviet-era spies were in the game.

So, the Russians were not playing around. Although one thing bothered me, why did MI6 need our help so desperately? It didn't make any sense, they had the same resources we did, something wasn't right. And we were right smack dab in the middle of it. If this gold train was so important, why was it being kept such a secret?

According to various reports on the train, the contents included gold, gold jewelry, jewels, diamonds, pearls, watches, around 200 paintings, Persian and Oriental rugs, silverware, chinaware, furniture, fine clothes, linen, porcelain, cameras, stamp collections and currency mostly US dollars and Swiss francs.

However, what struck me as odd was England was not known for its generosity. Just ask India, but that's for another day. But with that said, something was at play. Besides we'd been double-crossed so many times I didn't know who to trust anymore, nothing was what it seemed. So, we could have just been chasing our tails and didn't even know it.

Thinking back to the National Geographic special. I tried to figure out the current value of the contents. Supposedly, 28 tons of Nazi gold worth more than $2 billion was stashed on it. Eighty-pound gold bricks, diamonds the size of your fist, priceless artwork from Dutch and Polish painters were also included in the horde.

But nothing was ever found. They said a few years back, a couple of Polish researchers attempted to locate it. But the government and Poland wrote it off as a gimmick or publicity stunt.

Although there was one thing that did stick out, experts believed the trained contained booby-traps as well as a large amount of yellowcake plutonium. They believed it had seeped through its containers and protective shielding also rendering any treasure unobtainable. At least without developing severe radiation sickness and eventually succumbing to it.

So, why would they want it? None of it made any sense because even if they did find it, they wouldn't be able to use anything or give any of the valuables back to the rightful heirs.

It was all bull crap, all of it. Although I figured, to go through all this trouble to get to it, whatever they wanted must be worth it.

"Mom, what are you doing?" Emma snapped, as I buried my arm up to my elbow in the pot on the stove as instructed. My fingernails scraped the bottom of the copper pot as my casual turned desperate. Just as I was ready to give up, my fingers grazed something, something foreign at the bottom of the pot. Gripping it with my fingertips, I slowly raised the water out to the morning light that beamed through the small windows in the kitchen.

"It's a key, it's what the message said to look for, but I don't know what it unlocks. Or where we're supposed to find our next clue."

"You know, you'd think because they have a government to run, they'd have the stuff a little more tied up," Emma snapped, kicking over the broom standing by the icebox.

Suddenly, a wisp of light came in through a small crack above the front door, illuminating the side of the icebox. Neo-florescent paint became visible in the sunlight, spelling out the words 'Château Lamont.' Not sure what it meant, I grabbed Emma's attention.

"What do you think it means?" I asked, pushing the tattered curtains back so some more light could enter the room.

"Château Lamont. That's in Switzerland, it's that ski lodge I told you I wanted to go to, remember in the Swiss Alps? You said not less I hit the lottery, remember?"

I walked around the farmhouse, and to my surprise when I opened up a small closet that I assumed contained brooms and mops, found a pair of jackets identical to the ones we had just taken off and left in the field. However, in one of the pockets, was a Post-it notes from Eric. It read, "Hey Mom, these have the same features. And tell M I said hi. Love Eric."

"Hey M, here put this on. Your brother says hi and said these have the same features like the ones we already used," I said, handing her the solid white North face jacket. I quickly slipped my arms inside, as the cold was beginning to bite, and zipped it up to my chin.

"Hey Mom, there's a hoverbike out back, I think it's the same one we had before," Emma said, going out to examine it.

"Now, how do you know it's the same one?" I asked, following her behind the farmhouse.

"Because," she said, "I put this there," pulling a piece of gum off the back of the seat.

"I really wish you'd stop doing that, it's a disgusting habit. Do you not remember when your brother sat in gum? After you put some on that picnic bench, and it ruined his jeans."

"Mom, can you be a Mom later," Emma said and climbed up onto the large machine, she then turned the handlebars like she was driving it. "I want to drive, please. Can I, pretty please with sugar on top?"

"Well, I don't know, let me think about it for a second. Ah... No. Are you crazy?"

"Why not, I'm big enough. I can reach both buttons on the handlebars. If Disney World lets me ride the rides because I'm tall, why can't I drive this, there's no difference?"

"Sweetheart, you should really stop eating so many Froot Loops in the morning, they've gone to your head."

"You never let me do anything, you let Eric do whatever he wants," Emma said, throwing herself on the ground.

"Honey, can you save this temper tantrum for later. Maybe when we don't have a hundred trained killers after us. Hmmm?"

Pouting by the back of the machine, I realized her attitude was my fault as well as my ex-husband's as we had spoiled her since she was a baby and she was used to getting her way. But after sitting down next to her and calmly explaining why, she seemed to be okay with it.

Straddling the large flying machine, I nonchalantly pressed the up button after we had secured our seatbelts. And as like before, the craft rose into the sky. Bathed by the early morning sunlight, I twisted the throttle back gradually, giving us forward momentum. Checking out the red dot on the screen, that indicated us, I could see the machine was also pre-programmed like before, so as long as I kept the throttle compressed, we would be fine.

Coming up onto a large gaggle of geese, we flew beside them for a short time before they veered off to land in a pond. The "WHOOSHING" sound coming from the double blades, caused my eyelids to become heavy, but I shook my head to keep myself awake. I'd never been good in cars or planes because I could never stay awake.

So, to be on the safe side, I looked for the autopilot button again. After finding it, I had no hesitation this time before I pressed it. The green light on the dashboard lit up, indicating the autopilot had engaged. And we were on our way to ski on the Swiss Alps. It'd always been a dream of mine, to traverse the untouched landscape, while riding the pristine white waves of snow.

It wasn't long until I nodded off, I could feel Emma's head leaning against my shoulder, so I knew she was asleep also. The hum of the engines, helped me clear my head and allowed me time to think while I had a moment alone. Strangely, I wasn't scared though, it must've been all of the adrenaline, -fueling my mind off of it. But as I floated away, having an almost out of body experience, a strange sound caught my attention. What was confusing though, it sounded like a jet engine, and we were only at 3000 feet according to our altimeter which was dangerously low for an aircraft let alone a jet-powered one.

Shooting out of a patch of clouds, I saw the source of the sound. It was a jet pack. So, there was no way, we were gonna outrun this guy. I nudged Emma with my elbow and alerted her to our flying visitor.

"Who's that, are they on our side?" she said, using her free hand to rub her eyes.

"If I had to take an educated guess, I'd say no."

Fearing I would throw off the bikes balance, or navigation system, there wasn't anything I could do besides focusing on our flying friend and hope his actions didn't become hostile. But I wasn't going to hold my breath waiting.

"Hey Mom, those jet packs only have 30- or 40-seconds worth of fuel. He should be gone in a second."

I'm not sure how long it was, but just as she predicted, the man with the twin silver cylinders strapped to his back descended into the clouds. I hesitated before taking a sigh of relief.

The late morning sunlight helped warm us. But the frigid winter air still snapped at her heels as we sped through the sky like a sparrow. I could smell the snow in the air. So, I knew it was only a matter of time. Of course, I had to put the thought out of my head before the flakes started. They were small at first, but within a short time, they grew larger and our visibility dropped to nothing.

Only an hour had passed since the snow had started. Our windshield was proving to be no protection as we plowed through the raging blizzard. Eventually, we pulled our hoods up over our heads and pulled down on the strings. Shrinking the hole down small enough to where just our eyes, nose and mouth were exposed.

However, the conditions worsened by the moment. At this point, we had been airborne for two hours and 34 minutes according to the flight clock on the dashboard. But I was unsure how long it would take to get our location, and the snow was coming down so densely I couldn't see the dashboard to determine how much further we had to go.

Of course, naïvely believing it couldn't get any worse. Looking through the snow-covered windshield, I could see something directly in front of us. But it kept coming in and out of view. It wasn't until we got closer, I realized it was the base of a mountain and screamed at Emma, "HOLD ON!" Not sure why, there wasn't anything to hold on to or do except hitting the down button disengaging the autopilot. I attempted to steady myself and took a deep breath.

Placing my finger on the blue button, I lightly ran my thumb over the top of it, but just as I was ready to push it, I was persuaded not to by the machine, as it started to idle down like it did on the first trip when reaching its pre-programmed location.

Descending through the lingering clouds, we could see the ground below covered in fresh snow. The ski lifts were running at full capacity. The avid skiers enjoyed Château Lamont pristine conditions and trails, unaware of what was unfolding just above them. The machine came to a stop, resting its skis in the soft white billowy powder of the mountain.

Chapter Ten

Sliding off the piece of hardware that I was once terrified of, I checked out our surroundings. But as for outward appearances, it looked like a normal ski lodge with nothing out of place. However, I knew better than to trust my eyes, as I had learned that not everything is what it appears. So, we proceeded with caution.

We walked up to the concierge desk, leaving our airborne companion outside.

"Excuse me, do you speak English?" I asked, not remembering they did.

"Why of course, may I help you?" the meticulously groomed blonde-haired blue-eyed man asked.

After explaining we needed rentals, he pushed a small envelope across the desk. Without raising suspicion, I nudged Emma with my knee to get her attention.

I opened it, and read the contents. It was another clue, which read, "If sunlight is warm, then the owl's horn will be in the north."

"What's it say?" Emma whispered, looking over my forearm at the postcard size note.

"It's just another riddle. Why don't they just tell us, already? There's no need for all of this cloak and dagger bull crap."

"What the hell is that supposed to mean, if sunlight is warm?" Emma snapped, growing frustrated.

"For the love of all that's holy, will you please watch your language? You do remember, you are a child, right?"

"Sorry. But that doesn't make any sense, it's stupid. I want to go home; I don't want to do this anymore. I hate this place!"

Frankly, I didn't blame her because at this point, I wasn't a fan either. I mean call me crazy, but it was kind of hard to enjoy things when you were being shot at.

The Alpine territory of Switzerland, traditionally referred to as the Swiss Alps, is a major unique phenomenon of the country, and together with the Swiss Plateau in the Swiss part of the Jura Mountains, is one of its three main ecological zones. The Swiss Alps include both the Western Alps and the Eastern Alps, encompassing the region often considered as the core Alps. Almost all the highest mountains in the Alps are impaired by the rest of Switzerland.

Germany is to the north of Switzerland, Austria and Liechtenstein to the east, Italy to the south, and France to the west. People who have emigrated to Switzerland during their history have been using German, French, Italian, and Romansh. These are Switzerland's four official languages. The German-speaking people of Switzerland-about two-thirds of the population-speak Alemannic, which is considered to be a German dialect. Swiss people, however, write like people from Germany, and they even speak standard German very well.

Which means, it's well inside German territory. This also meant the Germans have their roving patrol of special ops. I'd read about them years earlier; they assisted the Swiss in patrolling the Alps and even helped with avalanche control on occasions.

So, I figured we should plan on running into them. Considering this was the peak season for avalanche control and they would be out in full force.

Walking out the front door, fixated on the envelope, I didn't notice the man brush up against me but rather felt him. However, when he said, 'Excuse me,' it was in Italian, but with a Russian accent.

"That didn't take long," I said to Emma, pulling my hood back over my head to cover my face. Taking my cue, she copied me and tightened the drawstrings so tight I could only see her eyes. Which of course, caused me to laugh. "You sure add levity at just the right moment," I said, patting her on her fake fur-lined hood.

Cautiously we walked up to the ski stand and requested two pairs, since we weren't registered guests of the hotel, they requested Swiss francs or US currency as payment. Knowing I didn't have any money, I began to protest before Emma pulled a large wad of cash from her pants pocket.

"Where are you getting all of this money, what did you poop a leprechaun?" Which of course, was the wrong thing to say to my easily amused daughter because it caused her to burst out in laughter, telling me to stop or she would pee her pants. Like at this point it would make a difference, but after regaining her composure, we proceeded to the ski lift, we caught the first set of chairs up the mountain.

But something was off, it was all too easy. I looked at the chairs behind us, and I saw why I had an uneasy feeling. It was occupied by two men in dark sunglasses and long jackets that appeared to be completely out of place from the normal attire. One of the men showed me the barrel of a gun and pointed down. "Yeah, sure that's gonna happen," I thought, whispering to Emma.

"At least the sunlight is on us, and I'm not freezing anymore."

"What did you say?" I asked Emma, pushing her to repeat herself.

"I said at least the sun's warming me, why? Mom has the altitude started to get to you?"

"What? No. Look at that mountain right there, it looks like a horn, doesn't it? Right there, see it," I reiterated, pointing off to the left of the lift to three mountains, the center one, was the one I was referring to.

That's why they said if the sunlight is warm. The note said, 'look for a horn'. And that mountain looked so much like a horn, it could have been on the New York Philharmonic. Of course, getting to it would be a whole new challenge because it was in the no go zone, where they were conducting avalanche control. And by what I knew of what that was, I didn't want any part of it. It consisted of the guys flying around in helicopters dropping high explosives into giant snowdrifts causing controlled avalanches. This way they wouldn't come through on their own, wiping out small villages as they go.

I also recalled reading about a mythical dwarf of Swiss and French folklore. Barbegazi is a creature of Swiss and French mythology. Referring to a variety of elves or fairies, a barbegazi looks like a small white-skinned guy with a big beard and massive feet.

They live in the mountains and ride in the mountains by skiing with their huge feet or using them as snowshoes.

They are rarely seen, partly because they spend their time in caves and tunnels when there is no snow around, and not before the first snowfall, and partly because they seek high elevations and cooler temperatures. Often, they help the shepherds to gather up missing sheep, and sometimes they try to dig up people who have been trapped by avalanches, to save them.

"Mom, let's get off now I have an idea," Emma said, slipping off the pole onto the freshly packed snow.

Making sure our skis were secure, we began to ride the white wave of flurries down the slope. Hoping we got to the end, unabated. However, the Gods of wishful thinking were not on my side. Two snowmobiles jumped a snowdrift and landed just feet from us. The drivers were dressed in white snowsuits and donned automatic weapons. Waving their barrels at us, they motioned us to stop.

Knowing what this meant, Emma leaned down into her skis, causing her rate of descent to increase as she raced down the mountain. I quickly followed suit, and my knees hunching over just slightly enough so I would gain further momentum.

However, even at full speed, I could tell we were not going to outrun them. So, alerting Emma she once again yelled, "Follow me, I have a plan."

Swaying from side to side, she did her best to avoid the gunfire and snow machines as they raced towards her like a pair of sharks coming in for the kill. But at the last moment, she turned to the right, and for a minute lost them. Of course, this win was short-lived as the whining engines of the snow machines struggled to get back on the slope. As the deep snow in which they had landed was difficult to maneuver.

By the time I got up beside Emma, I saw where she was headed. A deep crevasse, seven to 800 feet straight down. "You better hope these parachutes open, young lady, or you're grounded," I said, as we deliberately flew off the mountainside, again hovering for what seemed like an eternity in the air before our parachutes deployed and allowed us to float.

The snow machines couldn't stop in time, and both went over the cliff, landing in the rocks below, followed by a fiery explosion.

I don't know who thought it was a good idea to parachute in the middle of the winter. However, I can tell you first hand, it's not the most intelligent idea because once again, I couldn't feel my nose, cheeks, or really anything on my face. Although my offspring didn't seem to have a problem with it, which made me realize exactly how old I was. But I'll save that depression for another day.

Emily glided her parachute into the crevasse next to the base of the horn shaped mountain. At least my landing this time didn't consist of a basketball-sized pile of cow crap, which, you know is always nice.

"Hey Mom, do you hear that?" Emma said, untying her hood strings to expose her ears.

"I do, what is that? I didn't know Switzerland got earthquakes."

"I don't think that's an earthquake Mom, I think we might've set off an avalanche. Look for a plume of white, that's the telltale sign of one." Immediately, we began scanning the area, but couldn't see anything.

"I don't see anything," I said, realizing I'd spoken too soon. As I looked to my right, about a mile away, there was a football field size plume of white powder billowed in the air like a locomotive, powered by snow.

Initially, I figured we could get out of the way of the avalanche, and seconds away from clearing the front side of it in safety, I figured we were okay. But it caught the back of my skies and carried Emma and I, 30 feet down the mountain.

I underestimated the situation, as we plummeted down the mountain. My initial thought was that it would be hard to find my skis in this mess. I didn't know what was, which way was up or down, and I just listened for it to end, so I could pull away from its churning field of debris.

Then it came to an end, and it was completely black. I knew this was a very bad situation, and knew we had to work ourselves out. I had Emma's pant leg out in a hurry. I attempted to push my hands out, but I couldn't move either hand whatsoever. The snow was like a white tomb encasing us alive.

Suddenly, I remembered gravity and spit. Thank God, I was right side up, as my saliva dribbled down my chin toward the waiting snow. It was in that moment that I began to panic. I began to hyperventilate but soon gained control of my breathing, understanding that our only hope was that someone would dig us out before we went braindead.

I then made a concerted effort to use as minimal energy as necessary. But I felt my hands getting weak, and my head light. I prayed to God I wouldn't pass out, but apparently, He didn't get the memo. because the next thing I knew, my face at the snow in front of me felt like a ton of bricks.

In and out of consciousness, I saw what would appear to be children, digging us out. But I couldn't stay awake long enough to tell for sure, then something burned my nose. It was a horrible smell, but I started to come to and looked around for Emma. I saw her, she was sitting up beside me talking to one, but it's facial features were still indistinguishable because of the haziness and fog I was still in. However, after a couple of moments, I regained my eyesight.

There were three men, with short stubby legs, dressed in caps, and what appeared to be heavy handmade clothing in a collage of colors. But she didn't appear to be scared, or fearful which helped put me at ease as well. So, after sitting up slowly, and doing a visual check of Emma I asked, "How did we get here, and who are you?"

"Why were you skiing so far off the trail? Are you trying to get yourself killed, they have the trails marked off for a reason," the 3 1/2-foot man said, stoking the contents of the wood-burning stove near the corner of the quaint cottage they had brought us to.

"Are you the Barbegazi?"

"Seriously, you're asking me if we're elves? Do I look like a FRICKEN elf, lady? I'm a dwarf, and before you ask, I don't ride a unicorn, I don't have special powers and I can't help you find the pot of gold at the end of the damn rainbow. So, did I answer all of your ridiculous American questions?"

"Mom, that's racist. They prefer little people or dwarfs," Emma said, nodding with them in agreement.

"I'm sorry. I didn't mean to offend you. I guess I took a pretty good blow to the head."

"Well, all right. I'll let it slide this time. Name's Igor, that's Belarus, Vigor and...Kevin."

"Nice to meet you. Thank you, for saving me and my daughter. That was very kind, can I give you some money or something?"

"What exactly do you think we could do with money. All of our expenses are taken care of by the Swiss government. During avalanche season, we help patrol the high-risk areas, so dimwits like you don't get buried alive and are found during the spring thaw."

"I'm sorry, I thought little people were supposed to be friendly."

"Oh, you think so? Does it look like I have blue skin? Do you see me dancing around a chocolate factory like a blithering idiot? No, I'm not. So, get that stereotypical vision out of your head. You think its easy walking in three feet of snow when you only stand 3'5"? No, it's not. It's like snorting a blizzard."

"I apologize, I guess I did label you and I'm sorry," I said, trying to stand up but losing my balance.

"Where's the key, you still have it don't you? For crying out loud, please tell me you didn't lose it?"

"Even you know about the key and the map?" I asked, cupping my face to whisper?

"Why are you whispering? Everybody knows, now. Do you have the key still or not, it's a yes or no question? Time is of the essence," Igor said, sitting in a rocking chair next to the fireplace.

"I think so, but I'll check," I said, burying my hand in my pocket. "Here," I said, placing the key in his well-aged hand.

"I don't want it. I just asked if you had it. This is all on you sister, can you walk without passing out. Is if you fall on me, you'll crush me with your huge frame."

"Hey, be nice. I don't have a huge frame."

"Yeah, you keep telling yourself that lady. You see that wall, walk up to it, and put the key in the hole."

Reluctantly, I did as instructed and slid the key into the slot. And out of habit, turned it to the right first, but when nothing happened, I went back to the left and that was when the rock became light as a feather and spun around, displaying a small crevice behind the wall. There was a narrow tower of stone four feet high with a small leather bag on top.

Chapter Eleven

"Is that the map?" I asked, hesitating before approaching it? I'd seen enough Indiana Jones movies to know what would happen if I moved something that wasn't supposed to be moved.

But, after getting visual confirmation from Igor, I snatched the satchel off the tower and loosened the moose-hid strings that bounded it closed. But my excitement was short-lived when one of Igor's men said, "We got company, and it's not the cast from the sound of music."

"Good Lord, lady is there anybody that's not after you? Okay boys, you know the routine, get them through the tunnel and get ready to fight."

Hearing essentials to my spine because by the sound that was resonating from outside, it appeared there were four, maybe five snowmobiles. So, I knew it was only a matter of time before a large firefight ensued, and I didn't want Emma anywhere around it. The snow cave spiraled around, finding its way deep underground.

Trying to traverse the passages, some almost too narrow to pass through, we managed to shadow our guide. But at one point, feeling his erratic speed was done intentionally. So I reminded him, that we did not know the cave system as well as he and if we got lost, it would be on his conscience.

My guilt trip seems to work, as he slowed his pace to a snail's crawl. But gunfire could be heard behind us and it didn't appear too far off, which by now, I had become accustomed to. How crazy is that?

"Hey, where are you going? You can't just leave us here, we don't how to get out of this," I snapped at the tiny stranger.

"I'm not leaving you anywhere, but you can find your way out. For God's sake walk 100 feet and take a left, geez," he said, before running back to assist his associates.

Of course, he was right, after only walking a few feet, and taking the first left, we came out on the other side of Horn Mountain. I'm not sure if that was the name of it are not, that's just the nickname I gave it because of its shape. Through all of this, my curiosity was about to eat me alive. I had to find out what was inside the map.

Carefully, I untied the 70-year-old Rawhide lashings that secured the pouch shut and pulled the folded document out into the sunlight, which it hadn't seen since being put behind that wall by the last person that touched it. Most likely, a high-ranking member of the SS or Gestapo. The paper the map had been written on, was thick with a heavy fiber, so it opened up without any damage or tearing. Although in the scheme of things that didn't matter considering I didn't know what I was looking at, so I showed Emma.

"I'll take a picture, see what Eric thinks," she announced, before pulling her phone from a zip pocket on her jacket.

"You have a phone? Are you serious, all this time and you have a working phone?"

"Yeah, so I figured we need it," Emma said, taking multiple snapshots, before sending them to Eric in an encrypted file.

"Who are you?" I said, pleasantly surprised.

"What, you're always telling me, 'Be more responsible. So, I don't know why you're mad."

 "But .... What happened to playing with Barbies and baking chocolate chip cookies?"

"I still like that stuff, there's a time and place for it."

On one hand, I was happy that her maturity was shining through. However, on the other hand, it made me sad, my baby was growing up.

"Hey Mom, Eric says he knows where this is that he was able to match it up with some satellite maps NORAD took of the area a couple of months ago. He says it's in Poland, at the foot of Owl Mountain."

"Well, that would fall right in line with the clue. It said the owl. Hence Owl Mountain."

But the Swiss weather was not cooperating. The snow was beginning to fall again, and I could tell it was going to be a bad night if we got stuck out in it. So, my first thought was whether we should move away from the cave or not because it may be our only safe haven if the weather got worse.

"I don't suppose your brother, can tell us how the hell we get out of here," I said, wiping the snow from my cheeks and eyelashes.

Staring at the clouds rolling in, I knew we didn't have much time before they opened up and dumped on us. But that wasn't the only thing plaguing my mind. What would happen if our ill-tempered allies couldn't hold the bad guys off, where would that leave us? I had to keep telling myself, it wasn't dangerous what we were doing because if I didn't, there was no way in God's green earth we would have been out here.

But in some ways, it was considered an honor, to protect our country in such a way, of course, it was a thankless job since no one would ever know we had a hand in it.

The wind began to pick up, and in the flurries grew thicker before blowing horizontally.

"GEEZ! Do they ever have nice weather here, for criminy at Christmas I'm so sick of snow? We had to fly through the snow, we fell through the snow, we had to walk through the snow. I would just love one part of this journey not to involve cold weather and snow. Just once, that's all!"

"Mom, are you okay?"

"What? No, not really. I just can't stop thinking, last week my biggest problem was trying to figure out how to make a new meatloaf that you and your brother would eat. Now, I'm trying to ward off Russian spies while finding some Nazi treasure."

"Yeah, but how cool is that? We get to find buried treasure! That's awesome!"

"Well, I'm sorry I can't share in your enthusiasm." Looking down threw me off my game, as on the path in front of me, I saw footprints. "Hey Emma, can I ask you a question? What type of wildlife does Switzerland have?"

"Why, what are you looking at? Let me see," she said, stepping in front of me to examine the pawprints in the two-foot deep snow.

She stared at them for an awfully long time, which immediately was a cause for alarm. Although after measuring one the footprints against hers she paused. "Huh... I didn't expect this."

"Can you fill me in on the secret honey?" But she didn't respond which honestly terrified me more than annoyed me. "Hello, is my daughter in there?"

"Well, I think I know what it is. But you're not going to like the answer, I'm just warning you now," she said, stopping momentarily and pursing her lips together, "a brown bear, and if I had to guess four maybe 500 pounds."

"I thought bears hibernated, what happened to that? Has the whole world gone crazy?"

"She's probably looking for food, but you're right, she shouldn't be awake yet. I think the warm weather might've woken her up."

"You call this warm; I blew my nose a second ago and icicles came out."

"I don't have enough time to explain, Mom. Just keep your eyes open, because these are fresh which means she's still in our vicinity. You have any rounds left in your .S.T.O.P. gun?"

"No. I used the last one on those knuckle-dragging Neanderthals back in the tower. How about you, anything?"

"Nope, clean out," Emma said, retrieving her G.L.A.S.S. device from her satchel.

Placing her thumb on the top corner as she was instructed to by Eric back in England, she powered the device up. The bright blue screen lit up the flurry of flakes that encased us.

"What are you looking for, don't you think this is a bad time to check your email?"

"I'm not checking my email, Mom. Will you just stop for a second? I'm trying to see how far away we are from the Château."

"Why don't you just call them. They'll send someone down to rescue us."

I was able to see my daughter was irritated, I wanted to retreat so quickly, so I stood down from my original idea. She and her brother have always been tenacious, never taking no for an answer and always getting themselves out of impossible situations. So, I figured this was nothing different, and if I wanted to play the game, I had to play by their rules. And that meant never giving up, and never leaving anything undone. After my epiphany, I apologized, as I could see she was still upset.

"I am sorry. But you have to admit, this is some intense stuff. Currently, we're being stalked by a bear in the middle of a blizzard. Not to mention a couple of hours ago, we were buried under a couple of hundred tons of snow. I'm not as resilient as you, I don't have the energy or stamina like you do to keep this up. I don't want to hold you back, I don't want to hold your brother back, the only reason I even enrolled us in this is that I wanted us to be a family again."

"Well, as the saying goes, a family that dies together stays together," Emma said, with a giggle, throwing a handful of snow at me.

"Oh, that's lovely. Sounds like something you'd see on a gravestone. But I'm serious, I am sorry, but I did it for the right reasons. I just wanted us to spend more time together."

Before I finished my speech, the trees to the right of us snagged our attention. We could hear twigs and branches breaking, assuring us whatever it is had to be large in stature in order to make the noise it was making. I grabbed Emma by the back of her hood and gently began to walk her back toward me. I looked on the ground for a couple of rocks, as I read that if you make noise and let them know that you're there, bears will generally runoff.

However, this was a brown bear. Fearing humans weren't built into its DNA as it was an apex predator and feared nothing in heaven or earth. Weighing in at almost 500 pounds, there aren't many things the brown bear can't kill or dominate.

These omnivorous giants appear to be solitary creatures, except for females and their cubs, but occasionally they coexist. Spectacular gatherings can be seen in key Alaskan campsites as salmon swim downstream for summer spawn. In this season, thousands of bears will assemble to gorge on the fish, searching for fats that will fuel them through the long winter ahead. Throughout the autumn, a brown bear will consume as much as 90 pounds of food per day, and it may weigh double that well before hibernation as it does in the spring.

Experts suggest a way of doing this is smashing a couple of rocks together. The sound of them banging would scare them off. Of course, this one was hungry. So, I figured it could go either way. We could either become a two-piece meal or get away unscathed. It was a tossup.

I desperately searched the ground for a pair of stones or anything we could use as a weapon. But through the blinding snow, I couldn't see anything, we could just barely see the tree line. However, my fear was the bear could and we wouldn't even know it was there until it was on top of us.

I urged Emma to look through her bag, telling her to look for anything that could be used as a weapon. Then it dawned on me. The gold pen! I quickly devised a plan in my head to fend off our would-be wild attacker. But the rustling inside of the tree line, that it garnered so many minutes already of our attention grew silent. And for a moment, we thought we were safe. However, the hushing sound of the falling snow lulled us into a false sense of security because before we know it, the giant animal burst through the trees like an explosion.

Instantly rearing up on its hind legs, it let out a bloodcurdling roar. Swinging its head side to side, I could tell it was agitated. Of course, it was impossible to tell why. It could be it was mad we were there or because it was hungry. However, I didn't want to stick around and find out. Backing up slowly so as not to trip, we tried to reach the mouth of the cave. But before I knew it, it was on top of me, it felt like somebody had dropped a refrigerator on me.

Struggling to stay conscious, I covered my face and head with my hands and arms trying to fend off the mammoth beast. Emma's screams filled my ears as I fought for my life. Remembering the pen, I reached in my top right-hand coat pocket and pulled it from its case. I could only hope it would work, as I had to remove my hands and arm from my head and face, losing my only protection to stab it. I figured once I got close enough, I would have to use all doses until it was dead.

I figured it was now or never. So, I lurched up with all of my might and ran the pen through the beast's skin, penetrating its flesh, clicking the button as instructed. I prayed it would be enough to stop the animal's ferocious attack. But, after a couple of moments, my faith began to fade. Just as I was about to give up hope, its limbs stopped flailing about and suddenly its head tilted to the side. After a couple of seconds, it fell backward. It was dead and even though she was terrified, and crying hysterically, Emma was safe.

Unfortunately, I was a bit worse for wear, as the bear had gotten me several times in the arm and back with its claws and teeth. My blood quickly seeped through the white jacket, and I began to feel lightheaded. When I awoke, I was in a strange room I'd never been in before. People were tending to me, but I didn't recognize any of them.

But I heard a familiar voice, "Emma!" I yelled out.

"You're wake, I was so worried about you. Don't ever leave me, Mom," she said, wrapping her arms around my neck.

"Where are we?" I said, trying to sit upright. "It doesn't look familiar."

"We're in a safe house. Agent Nichols got us here. I used my S.P.O.T. and they were here within minutes. Too bad they don't deliver pizza." she replied. However, out of character for Emma, she leaned in and whispered, "Eric knows where the train's located."

"What, how is that possible by just looking at a picture of a map?"

"I don't know, he's your son you ask him," Emma said, blowing a large bubble with the bubble gum she acquired.

At first, I didn't feel the pain, at least until it radiated through my body like a hot spear as I tried to shift my torso. I knew my injuries had side lined me and made me useless to anybody in the field who would need my help. This included my kids. As I was having a pity party, my daughter jumped on my bed.

"I'm sorry I let you down," I said, feeling guilty.

"What are you talking about, you didn't let me down. Mom! You killed a 500-pound bear, with a ballpoint pen. That's amazing! I just wish I could tell my friends at school about it. Jenny McCarthy always brags that her dad is in the Peace Corps."

"Excuse me miss, you have a phone call," an attractive male nurse with blonde hair and blue eyes announced, pointing to my hospital room phone hanging on the wall next to the bed.

"Hello," I said, still groggy from the pain medication.

"Hey, there Smiley."

"Tom, oh my God. How did you know I was here?"

"Oh, I've got my ways. I heard you killed Smokey, I knew you had a little Rambo inside of you. How are you feeling?"

"Like I got ran over by a Mack truck. Besides that, I'm good. Where are you at, are you gonna be able to visit?"

"Afraid not, duty calls and all of that. But I'll check in on you from time to time. Okay, you and the kids stay safe, we'll talk again soon. Oh, tell the brat I said hi," his rugged and masculine voice echoed through the earpiece of the hospital phone before the call ended.

Chapter Twelve

"Is that Tom? I want to talk to him," Emma said, trying to pull the phone from my hand.

"He's gone honey, but he wanted me to say hi."

"Really, he said that?" she beamed.

"Well, kind of, technically said, "tell the brat I said hi.'"

"That was him, where is he at, did he say? Is he being held down by gunfire in the Congo or wrestling alligators in Australia?"

"What? No, I mean I don't know. He just said duty calls. Honey his job is like ours, he can't send us postcards from wherever he goes."

I don't know what kind of pain medication they were giving me. I couldn't feel a thing, not even my tongue. I think my looniness must've been getting to Emma, as she stepped out of the room while I was staring at a glass swearing it had moved.

Of course, by the time I came to, she was gone. She left her phone in the pocket of my hospital gown and had written on the palm of my hand, 'love you Mom.' I wanted to cry because I had come so far and now, I couldn't finish. Still, I had confidence in my children, and that was all that was important. Or at least that was what I kept telling myself, I guess I was trying to make myself feel better. But it wasn't working because all I could think about was Eric and Emma out there alone facing the Russians by themselves.

It was almost too much to bear. Suddenly, Emma's phone rang and pulled me out of my depressive state. "Hello," I answered, but carefully since I didn't know who was waiting on the other end.

"Hi Mom, it's Eric. M said you kicked a bear's butt. You okay, I heard he got the best of it?"

"Oh yeah, I kicked Smokey's furry little hinny," I said trying to hold it together, but after a couple of minutes, I couldn't and started laughing. "I'm sorry honey. I shouldn't laugh, but they've got me on such a strong dose of pain medication."

"That's okay, you don't have to apologize. I don't want to keep you on the phone too long, but I just wanted to tell you how proud I am, you saved Emma's life Mom. That takes some guts," he highlighted, knowing it would make me cry.

"Thank you, honey. That means so much to me," I said, breaking down in tears.

"Well, listen you need your rest. I don't want to drain your battery. But I'll call you again tomorrow, okay, and don't worry about Emma, she's a smart girl. I love you; I'll talk to you tomorrow."

"I love you too honey. You two be careful, okay, and give Emma a big hug for me. Bye Eric."

Knowing they would be okay helped me relax, a little but not much. It was still hard, I wanted to be there for them. Although according to them I already had been, which let me rest a little easier. But that night, I relived the bear attack all over again. In my dream, I could feel its hot breath and the smell of rotting meat coming from its mouth. Its teeth were as long as my thumb and its claws resembled jagged razor-sharp knives.

I tossed and turned, thrashing around in my bed. But in my dream, I was running, holding Emma and looking for any safety I could find. But the bear was relentless, hunting me down like a mystical predator... With every step I took, he was behind me, smashing limbs with his head as he bulldozed through the forest. Snorting, and growling every few feet, he would come up behind me and swipe at me with his 10-inch paws, tearing at the back of my shirt. I could feel the burning sensation of his claws penetrating my skin as he tore through my flesh.

Jerking myself awake, I laid there for an hour in my sweat-soaked bed. Barely able to move and still bogged down with fear, I reached for the nurse's call button hanging on the side of my bed.

"Yes," the nurse answered, bringing the box to life. "How can I help you?"

"Um... I just had a bad nightmare; can you send someone in just to sit with me for a few minutes?"

"I'll see what I can do, would you like a sleeping pill in the meantime?" the pleasant, but caring nurse's voice asked.

"Oh, no. I think I'm good on the sleeping area for a while. That last nightmare put an end to that, I will take some juice preferably grape if you have any."

"Sure, let me see what we've got in the fridge. I'll be right in, all right."

Just having someone sit with me helped. Like when I was a girl and I had a nightmare, my mother would always sit with me until I fell back asleep. I slung my legs over off the side of the bed and stared at the floor for a couple of minutes. I was trying to make up my mind, if I was going to attempt to walk over and look out the window as I'd been stuck in the bed for hours and was tired of looking at the same thing. However, my nurse walked in, and helped take that choice away by instructing me to get back in bed.

Taking a couple of sips from the paper cup that she had handed me, filled with grape juice, I started to relax again, but something was keeping me on edge. I kept telling myself they would be okay by themselves, but I just couldn't convince myself enough to relax completely.

"Eric, it's Emma. I'm on my way to checkpoint A, is everything in place?"

"Yeah, ETA 27 minutes. Remember, don't touch anything after you climb on. I'll be remotely operating it from here."

"I know Eric, God! You've told me a billion times, already. How can you do that anyway?"

"I installed four cameras. One for each angle. So, I'll see what you see, trust me. How's Mom, any better?"

"Well, the doctor said if she would've gotten bitten just an inch above where she did, she wouldn't make it."

Reluctantly, Emma sat on a rock next to a large pine tree that towered above her head. The snow was relentless, cutting her vision down to less than three feet. Emma stared up fixating on the gray and black angry clouds congregating just overhead. As the avalanche fell from the sky, unexpectedly, pea-sized hail started falling in between the sleeves of heavy snow. The hailstones clattered to the ground like marbles spilled from a box.

The sparse light seemed to dance on top of the snow, making it glitter when the sunlight hit it like a disco ball.

As I thought back to the memories of my youth, I distinctly remember a particular winter afternoon at my grandma's home. It was a really cold day, I remember, I was wrapped in two pairs of long underwear, two bulky sweaters, a thick fleece jacket, and my hot purple snow boots. I was about Emma's age, and winter snow was pure beauty to me.

When I walked out onto my grandma's back porch, I remember losing my breath, not just because of the freezing cold, but also because of the mesmerizing sight. I was instantly flabbergasted by the view. The entire field, as far as your eyes could see, was covered in a dense blanket of pure white.

Trying to extend my arms and legs as far as they could, I started making a snow angel. I could feel the impact of wet earth going through the gloves on my face. I got up from the ground to peek at the art, and just next to my angel wings, I found tiny animal paw prints. Interested to know what it was, I was ready to explore right away.

I went to trace the paw prints across the perimeter of the yard and came across the perpetrator. I noticed my grandma's dog, Rosy, just several feet away, jumping into the air in a futile effort to catch snowflakes in his mouth. The footprints were undoubtedly his. In love with the unusual weather, I closed my eyes to the sound of the day. I listened carefully.

The noise was so profoundly calm. Silence, there was still a lot to hear. I heard the scarce foliage moving softly in the wind. In the field, I heard a bird sing its song of joy. I heard the snapping of Rosy's teeth together through another botched effort to taste the dropping snowflakes.

Giggling, I heard the pattern of his legs against the snow as he raced happily. Suddenly, the sound of the back-door opening snapped me out of my haze. My grandma was standing in the doorway to reveal that supper was set. She'd been preparing soup. It was at this moment that I felt my stomach rumble. I was so caught up discovering the snow that I didn't notice my appetite. I could smell the hot fresh baked bread on the stove with the door ajar. I missed those days. However, reality came slamming back like a freight train, as I worried about Eric and Emma's safety.

"Eric, I see it," Emma announced, stepping a few feet back so the machine would have an unobstructed spot to land. The familiar sounds of the blades cutting through the cold air gave her some solace as she had a feeling she was being watched.

However, another sound she was all too familiar with also became present. Snowmobiles. The whine of the engines echoed off the snow and the surrounding mountains. Finding its way back to Emma's ears. "Eric, we've got company. Let's do it big brother!"

"Roger that, get on, make sure you buckle up. I'd never hear the end of it if you fell off, so make sure you're in tight. Hold on M, here we go."

The nine-foot long hoverbike lifted off the ground, rising into the air as Emma put on her helmet and dropped her visor. "Any time, Pinhead."

"Mom told you not to call me that!"

"Yeah, cry me a river, Cinderella. Come on Eric, move this tin can," Emma said, watching the snowmobiles congregate below her around her former landing site.

But this time, there were six snowmobiles, not like before, and there were ten men instead of the six they had dealt with earlier. So, she soon noticed that the Russians were raising up their game, which could only mean that they were getting closer.

Rising above the clouds, and leaving the snow below, Eric gripped his remote-control console from his location in Perth Australia, and gently pushed the forward lever slightly at first and then all the way.

"How you doing M? It's not too fast for you, is it?"

"No, it's fine. Oh, hey, I meant to tell you. Mom was a serious badass with that bear."

"Oh yeah, what happened? Did it have cubs with it or something, normally they don't attack like that unless they have cubs?"

"I didn't see any. But then again, I wasn't looking, either. I gotta tell you bro I had my doubts we were going to get out of there alive because I've seen one in the zoo before, but man their massive when you get up close to one. I could feel the ground shake as he was walking up to us."

"Wow. That must've been big if it set off impact tremors. Well, I'm glad you two are okay because when the director told me, I didn't know what to think, I just didn't want to go to a couple of funerals."

"Yeah, well, Mom definitely surprised me. I didn't know she had it in her, it was pretty incredible...Um... Eric, we've got a problem."

What Emma was referring to, were the two figures, gunning jet suits, that were heading towards her at lightning speed from the clouds just off to her right. Suddenly, a bright yellow beam about six feet long shot past the hoverbike.

"ERIC! THEIR SHOOTING AT ME! HELP!"

"Okay, hold on M. I'm deploying the smoke shield. If they can't see you, they can't hit you."

Emanating from all sides of the machine, the dark black cloud of smoke encased the bike and its rider. But suddenly, out of nowhere music began pumping through the headphones built into Emma's helmet. "IS THAT THE THEME SONG FROM JAMES BOND?" Emma screamed over the roar of the engines and the howl of the wind.

"I thought it was only appropriate," Eric said, laughing as he maneuvered the joystick.

"You're going to get something nice for Christmas this year!" Emma said, now feeling like a real spy after Eric's release of music.

Flying over the vast mountain range, Emma could feel the machine putting her to sleep with its harmonic vibration. Trying to stay awake was impossible, as she had been awake for almost 48 hours straight.

So, after confirming with Eric it was okay that she slept, she put her head down on the handlebars next to the console, careful not to hit any of the buttons. And after just a couple of moments, she slipped into a deep sleep.

Noticing her biometrics had dropped, Eric realized his kid sister was asleep and that he was now responsible for her life. His hand delicately maneuvered the machine through the night sky. Staying alert, he was on his 10th red bull and was now considering coffee to stay awake. His handler and mentor Dr. Philippe Michaels, was a nice older man in his late 70s. But his theories on quantum physics and plasma harnessing never got old.

"Excuse me, Dr. Michaels? I need some coffee, I can't afford to go to sleep," Eric said, refusing to take his eyes off the 13-inch color monitor in front of him showing his sister's location.

The famous leaning Tower of Pisa was just now visible on the horizon. At this point, Emma had been asleep for almost five hours. Unaware of her surroundings, or location she rattled herself awake. Wiping the sleep from her eyes, she gripped one handlebar and looked over the windshield as the snow had finally stopped blowing.

Leaning Tower of Pisa, Italian Torre Pendente di Pisa, is a medieval building in Pisa, Italy, famous for the establishment of its foundations, which led to a leaning of 5.5 degrees about 15 feet from the vertical tower at the end of the 20th century. Consequently, extensive work was done to stiffen the tower, and its leanness was narrowed down to less than 4.0 degrees.

The bell tower, which started in 1173 as the fourth and final building of the capital's monastery chain, was built to be 185 feet tall and was built of white marble. Three of its eight floors were constructed before the rough settlement of the foundations of the building in the wet soils became evident. At this same time, war broke out between the Italian city-states, and construction had been stopped for almost a century. This pause allowed the base of the tower to settle and potentially saved it from an early collapse.

The foundations were reinforced by injections of cement filler and different forms of bracing and strengthening, but the structure remained subsided at a rate of 0.05 inch per year at the end of the 20th century and was in danger of collapse.

The tower was closed in 1990 and all the bells were silenced as engineers embarked on a major straightening project. The soil was siphoned from below the foundations, the lean was reduced by 17 inches to 13.5, feet the work was finished in May 2001 and the structure was reopened for visitors.

Pisa continued to flatten without any more excavation, until in May 2008, the sensors revealed that the motion had finally stopped, with a total improvement of 19 inches. Project managers have anticipated the structure to stay unchanged for at least 200 years.

It was a magnificent example of Italian architecture. It's every floor lit up, and gave her a feeling of celebration, as it were Christmas or Boxing Day. Emma's teeth chattering so long, her jaws as she tried to speak. But after rubbing them for a couple of seconds, and getting the feeling back, she asked the inevitable question, "Are we there yet? What time is it," before stretching her arms high above her head, carelessly putting herself in danger.

Chapter Thirteen

"It's 4:30 AM. I got it programmed to land about 50 feet from the leaning Tower of Pisa. Now, this early in the morning there won't be any security. But your window to complete your mission is narrow M. You have 22 minutes to get in get the other section of the map and get out undetected."

"I thought we had the map? Now there's another one, how many pieces are there?" Emma asked, becoming frustrated.

"Just the two, we have part one. But we need part two if we want to find the tunnel where the trains are located."

"I don't understand what the big deal about a train is anyway. Can't they just build another one, what's so special about this one besides the gold?"

"It's full of yellowcake plutonium. The most radioactive substance on the planet. We can't let the Russians get a hold of this; it would be a disaster."

"But I thought they already had nuclear weapons, why do they want the Betty Crocker stuff?"

"What are you talking about, Betty Crocker? Oh, yellowcake I get it."

"DUH... How did you get early acceptance to MIT, Rosie's smarter than you?"

"Look butt munch, I'll superglue your hand to your face again."

"Blah, blah, blah. Did you put the food on this thing, or don't they have meal service on this flight?"

"Yes, M. There should be some chocolate chip granola bars in the compartment by your knee on the right-hand side."

"Nice! Aw... You even put chocolate milk in here, okay maybe you're not as brain-dead as a tuna fish sandwich."

"Oh, my God, will you stop talking. I can't concentrate with you yapping in my ear. Now, as I was saying, 22 minutes M. Not a minute more, understand."

"Why, what happens if I stay longer?" Emma asked, riling up her brother.

"You'll have every gun-toting psycho from here to hell after you. Russians, Argentinians, Belgians, Chinese, you know there's a bounty on our head."

"What does that mean, a bounty? Is that like a reward, can we collect it?"

"No M, it doesn't work like that. It means people want us dead. Bad people."

"Oh, how much are they offering?"

"Well, I know Russia is offering 380 million rubles."

"How much is that in US currency?" Emma asked.

"About $5 million," Eric said, concentrating on the joystick and the GPS tracking system that was guiding her aircraft.

"Wow, they really don't like us," Emma said, shrugging off the international bounty.

Gradually, the MIT designed double-bladed aircraft came to rest a few feet from the visitor center near the tower Pisa. A flock of birds startled by the landing, who often a group before scattering around the statue of Michael Angelo sitting in the courtyard. The bell tower visible from Emma's position, caught her attention. A shiny object had glimmered in the early morning Tuscany sun. Considering the structure was made entirely of marble, she found this strange.

Stepping back off to the side to get a better view, she rifled around her satchel, until she found her spyglass at the bottom, sitting next to her last stick of gum. Concealing her handheld optical device, she focused it on the top floor of the tower where she had caught sight of the anomaly. As she expected, she saw the barrel of a gun but not the shooter themselves.

Slipping her helmet off her head, she took a step back and placed it on the seat of the aircraft, unwittingly severing communications between her and Eric. However, her predawn hours were about to get much more exciting. Suddenly, three men dressed all in black appeared seemingly out of nowhere.

Emma now in her fighting stance, prepared for battle. Leaning back out of the way, she avoided the first man's numb chucks as they swung so close to her face, it caused a breeze to move her hair. She spun around, and punched the second man in the groin with a reverse back punch. However, unaware of the third man's location, she dropped to the snow-covered ground and saw him running at her with a large knife.

Extending her arm as far as it would go, she grabbed the helmet from the seat. Using it as a shield, she disarmed the man, knocking the knife out of his hand. But now she was in full hand-to-hand combat with a full-grown adult. Something she had never done before, but she figured 'no time like the present' and prepared for a full-on roundhouse kick to his face.

Unexpectedly though, a pair of arms wrapped around her chest, and lifted her off the ground. Kicking her feet back, causing pain to her would-be abductor, he released his grip. However, this was only momentary, as the other two men regrouped and prepared to use flanking techniques. However, Emma noticed this and immediately went on the counter-attack, running over to the hoverbike. She used it as a steppingstone and landed her first kick into the first man's face, rendering him unconscious. The second man spoke in Italian, 'You will die little girl.'

"Not before you, ass hat," Emma said, doing a cartwheel and kicking the man in the face first with her left foot and then her right. Knocking the man to the ground, she had an idea of what to do next as she had remembered a special, she had seen on TV about the elasticity of pine trees. She noticed a dozen 12-foot saplings planted beside the visitor center in a row.

Running towards them, she managed to get hold of one of their trunks and scurried halfway up it. Shifting her weight away from the man, the tree started to bend. Suddenly, the Evergreen sent her back towards him at a high rate of speed. They fell to the ground after she crashed into him, but it wasn't enough. So, once she was sure he was unconscious, she stopped kicking and punching her motionless attacker.

The other two men staggered to their feet. Still disoriented by the brutal beating they had taken from the preteen; they ran off leaving their comrade behind.

Picking up the smashed helmet, she attempted to bring up Eric on the two-way radio, not sure if it would work or not. "Hey, are you there?"

"Yeah, I'm here, I wonder what happened to you. Everything, all right?"

"Un-huh, I think I sprained my pinky though. Hey, I'm hungry. How about some pancakes? Oh, and bacon too!"

"All right, I'll see what I can do," Eric said, getting up from his office chair and throwing the six empty cans of red bull on his desk into the trash can.

The Tuscany sky lit up like fire, its early morning sun-drenched the landscape around the tower. Tourists filled the once empty streets. The sounds of children and the laughter could be heard in the background as she walked around the area, attempting to look as inconspicuous as possible. She tried to distance herself from the attention the hoverbike was starting to receive and pretended she didn't know anything about it. Diligently, she waited for her brother's instructions, examining the giant leaning marble structure.

She glanced over her shoulder, listening to local residents telling the policemen she was the one who came down on the machine... Then the words she dreaded to hear permeated her eardrums, "Scusatemi perdere," which in translation is 'Excuse me miss' in Italian.

In a panic, Emma gripped her helmet tightly and began to run. Heading inside the structure, she ducked under the red velvet rope and ran up the stairs. Scared to look back, she remained focused on her next move. Unfortunately, she was unaware that the tower only had seven stories. Emma walked over to the observation deck and gazed out at the Tuscan landscape.

Coming up behind her, were the familiar voices of the policemen, who had chased her into the structure. Realizing she was trapped with no way out, she called out Eric for his assistance.

"Hang on M, look to your right. Do you see the pillar with a two-inch yellow on the bottom of it? Walk over to it, and stand directly behind it, then keep your hands to your side. Let me know when you're there."

"Okay, I'm here. Now what?" Emma said, hearing the policeman again. "Anytime, big bro whatever you're going to do, you'd better do it."

"Look to your right, you should see a rope and a harness. Get into the harness, and throw the rope over the side! Come on M, move, move!"

"Okay, I'm good. I'm going over," Emma said, tossing the 30-gauge horsehair rope over the side of the 190-foot structure.

Repelling down the rope like a monkey down a tree, she was out of the policeman's reach in seconds. Keeping her legs around it as she made a controlled descent, she noticed the rope came up 20 feet short. Now wearing her cracked helmet, she squealed into the headset. "Eric! The rope's not long enough, it doesn't go all the way to the ground!"

"CRAPNUGGETS! Okay, give me a second. M! On the second floor, there should be a long metal pole sticking out of the marble. Grab a hold of it, and pull yourself in, you got it?"

"Yeah, I see the pole. I got it...... Okay, I'm in, now what?"

"When you get outside run pass the tourist booth, it's just to the left of that, you'll see a pair of red Vespa scooters. When you get to on let me know."

Emma was shocked when she went up to the identical scooters.

"MOM? What are you doing here, you shouldn't be out of bed."

"Yeah, I know. But how many times when you guys get sick, do you stay in bed?"

"What's going on Emma?" Eric's voice echoed through his sister's headset.

"It's Mom!"

"Say again, I don't think I heard you right. It sounded like you said Mom's there," Eric replied.

"I couldn't let you guys do this alone," I said, trying to reassure my daughter.

Shaking her head in disbelief, Emma climbed on one of the Vespa's and motioned me to get another one.

"CRAP! Eric, I know you're getting tired of hearing this, but we've got company again. It's like a dozen cops."

"I know Emma, I hacked into the surveillance cameras. Get on the scooters, and go straight, until you get to Tuscany Square. There, you're going to want to turn right on the first alley. Follow that down until the dead end, then if you look to the left, you'll see a small doorway with stairs. Go down it!"

"You want us to ride down these steps, are you nuts. Do you not remember what happened when we taped Dad's manila folders to our feet? Then tried, skiing down our stairs!"

"Trust me, just do it!"

Coming to the dead-end, we could see the arched doorway Eric was referring to and slowly went down the stairs. Bouncing down the limestone blocks, they came out across the street from the statue of David at Tuscany's town square.

Thinking we were in the clear, we applied the brakes to the miniature motorcycles and stopped in the middle of the road, looking back to make sure we weren't followed. But just as I took a deep sigh of relief, a pair of black Austin Martens squealed around the corner. The headlight covered in the cars, popped up, exposing the barrels of 50 caliber submachine guns.

"Rat a tat, rat a tat.... rat a tat, rat a tat, ray a tat!"

"MOM! They're shooting at us!" Emma yelled, gunning the scooters throttle the full capacity.

"Eric, these things are too damn slow, we need more power," I yelled at Emma's helmet.

"Push the yellow button, and hold on!"

"HE SAID PUSH THE YELLOW BUTTON!" Emma yelled, pressing hers first.

The mere two-stroke engine began roaring like a Formula One race car engine. The speedometer went from 35 to 65 in two seconds. The statues that lined the road, whizzed by like mosquitoes hitting the car's windshield. But since the small engines weren't built to handle such stress, they began to smoke. Eventually giving out entirely.

Bluish black smoke poured from the aluminum crankcases. Pulling off the road into a field next to a couple of horses and a small barn, I switched off my ignition. Letting the Italian built engines rest, I checked out our surroundings. My shoulder was killing me by now. But after giving birth to two kids, it was nothing.

We walked over to the equestrians so Emma could pet them. She loves horses. At first, I thought I was hearing things, but the sound of helicopter blades chopping through the air filled my ears.

"Tenacious little things aren't they," Emma said, examining her scooter.

The Sikorsky UH 60 attack helicopter fell from the sky before it was a few feet from the ground, it came to a controlled stop. Landing just a few feet from our still smoldering scooters. The door of the intimidating attack aircraft came to rest on the ground.

"Good morning, I'm general Monahan of the Italian Army. You must be agent Elkin," the middle-aged man with a bushy mustache announced extending his hand.

Reluctantly, I grasped his waiting appendage. Keeping my eye on Emma, I could see she had that look again. She was like a human lie detector.

"Your government is very proud of you," he added, trying to convince me he was one of the good guys.

But something was off, and this time even I felt it. So, I let him do all of the talking, but continued to make sure I stayed an arm's length away.

"Do you have the map, may I see it?" the general asked, staring at me first, then Emma.

"Forgive me general, if I'm reluctant to trust you. But it seems like whoever's polite to us, eventually tries to kill us."

"Of course, that's to be understood, being a spy brings along inherent dangers. Now, may I see the map, you do have it?"

Unfortunately, during the general's line of questioning. A pair of soldiers dressed in military fatigues donning AK-47s, stepped from the belly of the aircraft, using their appearance to intimidate.

Shaking my head, I said, "No general, we sure don't, we did, but we must have dropped it. We were just talking about that before you dropped in unexpectedly."

Glancing over at Emma, her radar was going off, and she knew what I did.

"Tell me general, how much are you getting out of this? A couple hundred million, or is it the yellowcake. That's it, isn't it, you don't care about the gold you just want the uranium. What you gonna do with it general, wipe out a small country? Maybe start World War III," I said, intentionally antagonizing him?

<h1 style="text-align:center">Chapter Fourteen</h1>

"Why would you want to start a war?" Emma asked, leaning back against her scooter? "Isn't there enough war, already without you starting another one?"

"No, you have this all wrong. We are on the same team, on the same side. I do not want war, why would you say such a silly thing? I just want to see the proper people get their valuables returned to them, that is all. I have no nefarious reasons. Now please, give me the map, I will keep it safe. I give you my word."

"Oh, well, in that case."

"So, you do have the map. Yes?" the general said, growing frustrated.

"No. I told you we had it but lost it while we were being chased. Why is that so hard to believe, we've had everybody from here to hell after us."

"Well, that's disappointing to hear. Of course, forgive me if I have you searched, as people have been known to be dishonest with me in the past. But please, take no offense to it."

I knew this was not going to sit well with Emma. Making eye contact, she and I nodded at one another, giving each other a supplemental signal to immobilize the targets. Of course, my slow and sluggish speed was no match for her lightning pace, as she had already kicked the first soldier in the groin and while he was down, elbowed him in the face and disarmed him.

The general lunged for me, but I leaned back avoiding his grip. The second soldier came to the general's defense, but Emma took the opportunity to jump off the seat of her scooter and landed on his back squeezing his neck until he passed out.

It was now us against the general. Emma let out a shrieking, "HIYA!" kicking the general's leg out from underneath him, then repeatedly punching him in the face until he fell to the ground, moaning in pain. Assuring he wouldn't get up, Emma grabbed one of the AK-47s and knocked the general out with the butt of the weapon.

Although we relaxed too soon, as we had forgotten about the pilot. Observing what had transpired, he ran from the cockpit of the craft. He swung his eight-inch military issued service knife wildly through the air. Catching Emma on the tip of her right earlobe.

Looking at my child bleed, I snapped, and yelled, "YOU SON OF A BITCH! YOU CUT MY CHILD!" before leaping at the man still wearing his pilot's helmet. After that, I blacked out, however, when I awoke all four men were unconscious. Emma was sitting on the back of her scooter seemingly unaffected by everything, eating a granola bar.

"I was wondering when you were gonna come out of it. You want a granola bar? I got one left Mom."

"Are you okay honey?" I asked cradling her hand in my face.

"I'm fine. Stop," she complained as I kissed her repeatedly on the head and told her how happy I was she was okay.

"You know how to fly a helicopter?" I said jokingly, looking at the giant attack craft sitting dormant 100 feet from us.

"No, but what I do know is they were probably tracking his movements Mom. We should get out of dodge because they are going to be looking for him. And then they're gonna be looking for us. Hey Eric, where do we go from here?"

"Did you guys get, part two of the map yet?" his voice crackled over Emily's almost unrecognizable helmet.

"You never told us where we were supposed to find it," Emma replied.

"The general has it. Check his pockets, he's probably got it on him," Eric said, alerting us to the obvious.

I scoured all of his pockets but not finding it until I got to the very last one on the inside of his jacket. Pulling it from the lint riddled pouch, I carefully unfurled it. It was indeed the second part of the map. The one that would show the exact location of the fabled Nazi train of gold.

The air grew colder as we stood there conversing, trying to figure out our next move. The gray looming clouds that were once far behind us were now almost on top of us. We walked cautiously to the barn, noticing one of the double doors was open. Hoping we weren't walking into a trap; I announced our presence. No one replied, so Emma yelled in Italian, "C'è qualcuno qui," which in translation meant 'Is anyone here'? But she too got no reply.

Suddenly, I saw a shadow in the barn. I grabbed the back of Emily's jacket, gesturing her not to make any noise. Pointing at the shadow, we cautiously approached, tightening our fist for battle. But to our pleasant surprise, as we jumped in front of the door, leveling the barrels of our recently acquired AK-47s, we were met by a black pony that had a white spot on his forehead.

"Aw...he's so cute. I wonder why he's out here all by himself," Emma said, patting the pony's mane.

An avalanche of snow fell from the sky. The blinding snow made it impossible to see more than five feet in front of your face. The wind began to howl, blowing the snow through our open hoods down into are now sweaty cavities. I ushered Emma inside the barn, and enclosed the top door after lighting a lantern that was half-full of kerosene for warmth and light.

"What do we do now?" Emma said, still petting the pony.

"We can't take the scooters and we can't go out there. The temperatures dropping, feels like it's about 20. I think we should stay in here tonight, and ride out the storm. I figure if the conditions are too bad, the general's friends won't come looking for him until morning. By then we should be able to figure this out. Why don't you try to get some sleep, I'll push some of this hay around? It looks fairly new so it should be clean."

"You're not going to sleep with me, I don't wanna lay down by myself," Emma complained.

"Honey, one of us has to keep watch because they will come looking for him. Mark my words, they will. And we will be out manned and outgunned when they do. So, lay down and try to get some sleep. You're gonna need your energy," I said, kissing her on the forehead and brushing her blonde hair out of her eyes. "Emma, no matter what happens, I'm very, very proud of you. Sweet dreams."

Sitting there alone, occasionally staring out through the cracks of the loosely fitted door, I guarded our location like a mama bear. Every 30 minutes or so, I got up to walk around, trying to stay warm and would explore a little more each time.

I couldn't believe I missed those hoverbikes. But I figured anything that got me off the ground and out of harm's way would be better than being a sitting duck like we currently were. I tried not to think about the danger of what could happen if we got caught and tried to stay positive. It wasn't easy. Especially, since the larger than usual dose of pain medication they had given me before I slipped out of the hospital was wearing off.

Moving my head to the side, back and forth, I snapped my neck, and cracked my knuckles, hoping the extra movement would keep me alert. It reminded me of the time the kid's father and I drove from Tampa Florida to Georgia one weekend nonstop. I had to keep the windows rolled down, or I would have fallen asleep at the wheel.

I looked over at Emma, she was curled up in the fetal position next to the pony which strangely enough had laid down beside her like it was trying to lend some comfort to the chaotic situation.

The snow had managed to land for hours and hours. The trees were destroyed branch by branch and the hedges were destroyed. At this point, the blizzard seemed to be seen as a ruthless king seeking to lay an aerial assault as the region became buried by snow from top to bottom and left decimated like the Gaza Strip in Saudi Arabia.

I had too much time with my thoughts. That's never a good thing when you have unresolved issues. I felt rather guilty, because I knew damn well that leaving the hospital, put them in more danger than if I would've just stayed put. But I couldn't just lay there, wondering if they were okay.

I knew our relationship hadn't been the best since their father and I split up. But I truly did the best I could, however, divorce is never an easy thing. This I learned first-hand. However, I couldn't help wondering how my ex-husband would feel if he knew our kids were moonlighting as spies, out to save the world. Of course, it probably wouldn't go over well, just thinking about it was insane. Let alone carrying it out.

I figured it was too late for that as the time for worrying had passed.

A sliver of sunlight cascaded through the cracks in the barn door, alerting me dawn had arrived. We had beaten the clock. But I didn't know for how long. Cracking the top door open just enough to stick my head out, I managed to get a look around at the fresh fallen snow that encased everything in sight. The one thing I was looking for was gone, the helicopter was missing. But I couldn't figure out how, did I fall asleep. Is that why I didn't hear it take off? And if that was the case, why didn't the men come to the barn looking for us.

Unless they realized we took their weapons, and they were now outgunned. I figured, they would be back regardless and wouldn't be happy upon their return.

"EMMA! Get up, the chopper's gone and so is the general."

"What, how is that possible? I didn't hear it take off," she said, brushing the hay off her jacket.

"I don't know. But I've got an idea, give me a hand with the saddles," I said grabbing the well-built equestrian equipment from a hook on the wall it was hanging on.

"Are we gonna ride horses? This is the best vacation ever," Emma squealed with excitement.

"Um... Honey, you do realize this isn't a vaca... Never mind. Yes, were going to ride horses. Come over here and help me get this other saddle down. Be careful, it's heavy, I don't want it falling on you."

"Do you know how to put a saddle on a horse?" she asked, barely able to hold her side up as we maneuvered it to the ground.

"I do not. Then again 24 hours ago I didn't know how to drive a hover bike either. So, you live and learn. Now, all we have to do is get the horses to cooperate. That should be a neat trick," I said wiping the perspiration from my brow.

"How are you going to do that, they're pretty big Mom."

"Yes honey, I'm well aware of that, just stay here for a minute. I'm gonna see if I get one in the barn. I think it will be easier in here because we can stand on that little section of wooden fence right there."

Going out into the elements was not my favorite part of the morning. But it had to be done, however, to my horror I didn't see either of the horses. I wondered where they went because the snow had stopped enough that my visibility was pretty good. I could see across the field but didn't see the equestrians. Suddenly, Emma yelled, "MOM!"

Running back to the barn, I tripped over a rock and landed in the mud. I could've complained, but who would've listened. Trying to get as much off as possible, I finally got back to the door that was still slightly ajar.

"What's wrong? Oh, I wondered where they went, how did you get them in here?"

"Through the back doors, they just pushed their way through the bales of hay that were covering it. I guess they were hungry. I think they're trained too," Emma said, feeding one of the animals a handful of hay.

"Why do you think they're trained?" I asked stepping back expecting a display.

They didn't disappoint. Emma commanded them, "ow down."

The 1500-pound steeds amazingly bent their knees and handed Emma's waiting hand their heads. She offered them each a handful of hay. They pulled it out of the closed grip gently.

I poked my head back outside, half expecting to see something. But it was dead quiet. The only thing even remotely close to noise was the crisp dancing of the new snowflakes on the frozen snow from the night before. Still the chill in the air, wasn't enough to explain the tightness in my stomach. It felt like an instinct, trying to climb out of me.

Not able to shake my feeling of paranoia, I walked over to Emma. She was still feeding the horses, I instructed her to stay put while I took a look around. The barn door creaked as I pushed it open, almost blown out of my grip, by the howling wind that had still yet to subside. I watched the barren trees blow in the breeze, not even acknowledging the needle-like wind that burrowed through my jacket and into my skin.

The frozen snow crunched under my boots, with every step. I tried to retrace my steps, to leave less tracks. But the constant bombardment of fresh snow made that impossible. As the wind began to pick up to almost gale force, I knew my time outside was limited, and began to wonder of attempting to take the horses out in this climate was a good idea.

I kept thinking there had to be a better way, some type of safer route to our next destination. But nothing came to mind as I stood there, my teeth chattering. I honestly didn't know what to do because my training was scarce at best. At least what I remember of it, which was another question that plagued me. How much advanced training had I received that I was not aware of. I recalled a program the CIA had thrown together haphazardly back in the early 90s nicknamed Third Eye.

It was essentially designed to train unwilling candidates subliminally. They were given hours long movies to watch with encoded messages built-in to the framework that would flash every couple of seconds, giving the candidates skills beyond their comprehension. Of course, rumor had it, the program was dismantled. But I knew that what the government said and what the government actually did were always two different things.

By looking at the clouds getting darker by the moment. I determined we had one chance, and we needed to take it. Marching my way back through the snow, I ordered Emma to load up the horses, and to make sure they had enough blankets for travel.

Although by the time we got outside, after spending almost an hour loading the equestrians up, the wind had picked up to an angry mess of snow and hail. The pellets of ice were only a quarter inch at best, however, the fear remained, the size would increase over time. And we probably were too far away from the barn to reach shelter in time.

"Mom? Are you sure it's a good idea, we go out in this? It looks pretty bad out here, maybe we should try and wait it out," Emma said, tightening her hood again.

"We can't, the general's gonna be back, and is going to have reinforcements. We have two weapons, and by the looks of them, the Russian-made AK-47s are not known for their reliability." I pause for a moment and second-guessed my decision. The wind was now blowing the snow horizontally into our faces, and it was obvious the horses did not want to be outside. And as the saying goes "If an animal is smart enough to get out of the weather, then you should be to," but I couldn't see any other options available.

After only a few hundred feet, I spun around my saddle. But because of the driving snow I couldn't even see the barn anymore. So, we couldn't go back even if we wanted to, my lips had become so chapped, they were now cracked and bleeding from the howling wind that was relentlessly pelting us in the face.

We had been riding for almost two hours. Nothing was out there, or at least that wanted to be seen because with every step, the weather worsened, and my hope diminished that we would find safe harbor. I was at the end of my ropes when I heard Emma.

"Mom, there's something ahead of us. Look," Emma said, pointing to a dark mass a few feet in front of us but still disguised by the blizzard.

Chapter Fifteen

I couldn't tell what it was, it could've been a hill of dog crap and I would've known any different. It was a building, a warehouse of some kind. The outside was gray metal planking, but the roof was white and not just from the snow. However, as we got closer, we heard the "clank, clank, chuchink." Suddenly, the entire side of the building began to move, as a gigantic 30-foot door slid horizontally open, a burst of warm air shot out, engulfing the horses and us.

We were standing just inches away from warmth and comfort. We were hesitant to go any further, as we were unaware of who was offering us the shelter. There were no emblems or signs on the walls or door that I could see that would either warn us or discourage us from entering. However, considering what we had already gone through, my ability to trust was a bit banged up. So, I figured it was better to be safe than sorry.

"Eric," I heard Emma say. I figured she was starting to hallucinate from the cold, and at first didn't give it much merit.

It wasn't until I heard his voice, I believed the reality in front of us.

"Eric? Oh my God, I am so happy to see you son. How did you know where to find us?" I asked, starting to cry.

"One of you must've activated your "S.P.O.T" system. We picked up a signal last night, and here we are," he said, helping his sister off her horse.

I led both horses inside, and unbuckled their saddles. The door slid closed behind us reaching its final destination with a, "CLUNK" and "WHOOSH!"

For a moment, all seemed normal, Eric and Emma talked. I warmed my hands by a wood stove. The horses had fresh oats, and didn't fear freezing to death. So why was I uneasy, everything was working out. Everything seemed perfect, almost too perfect. I shushed Eric and Emma, telling them to keep their voices down while I listened.

I was hoping my ears were playing tricks on me, but I heard the voices again. This time clearly and they were speaking Russian. I tossed my weapon to Eric, and shrugged my shoulders. "You'll have better luck with that, then I will," I added, throwing him a handful of bullets I'd found on the ground near the chopper.

The voices sounded close. Now right outside the door. Startling all three of us, came a banging on the outside of the building and then a Russian voice ordering us outside or they'd opened fired.

But I played off Eric's expression because he appeared not to be concerned, as he didn't reply to their demands. Standing there in the open area under the warm lamps that hung from the ceiling, I took time to take inventory of my life, in case I didn't make it, or something happened. I had no regrets, I'd made mistakes. But I stand by them, and if that means dying beside my children. I was ready too, I just hoped it didn't come to that.

However, after a few moments passed, nothing happened. For all intents and purposes, we thought we were in the clear until we heard the words "FIRE!" come from multiple sources outside. I stood petrified, too scared to move. My legs felt glued to the floor as I waited for the barrage of bullets to ensue. But after another 10 minutes of silence, we knew something was up but were afraid to check. I looked at Eric for his approval, and he nodded as if to say, 'Do what you have to do.'

Suddenly, we heard five single gunshots. Then silence took over again. Terrified to even speak, none of us breathed as we waited for the inevitable. Although the only sounds that could be clearly detected through the thick metal plating, was the wind which in itself was barely distinguishable. So, at that point, I figured even if they were outside, we wouldn't hear them.

But I diligently stood by the door, not really sure what I'd do if somebody tried to breach it. I just figured it was the best place to stand, at least I looked tough. God only knows how much longer we stood there, motionless in the middle of this makeshift warehouse. It appeared to only be 50 minutes, but in my head, it felt like two hours. Finally, I had had enough, and waited as long as I could. I placed my hand on the large blue metal handle that was basically another strip of metal that ran down the length of the 30-foot-long door.

I gripped hold of the handle with all my might and pulled it upward. Waiting for some mechanical feature to assist, I stood there, momentarily staring at it like a caveman looking at a fire. Until Eric said, "It's not automatic, you've got to pull it open manually Mom."

He started to make his way over to help, and I raised my hand. "You stay with your sister, and if anything happens you get her out of here, understand?"

He nodded in agreement, which made me feel a little better but not enough to pull the door open. I realized I didn't have much of a choice, and pulled on it harder this time using my weight as a momentum. Surprisingly, it rolled fairly easily on its greased tracks. The wind hadn't stopped, and the snow was still coming down in sheets, to the point where it was blocking out the sun.

But I didn't see the general, or his entourage of soldiers. However, visibility was awful. Maybe 10 feet at best, so I wasn't confident they weren't out there. I turned around to step back to the entrance and glanced down by my left foot. It was fresh blood. I looked up at Eric, but didn't want to alert Emma. Though whispering in his ear, probably wasn't the best way to go to keep secrecy because she immediately chimed in and asked what I was whispering to him.

"What are you looking at, and why are you being so secretive and whispering?" she asked, looking down at the stain in its otherwise white surrounding. "Is that blood, did those guys get shot?"

"I don't know honey," I said trying to shield her eyes.

"Well, if they're all dead. Then who's he," Emma remarked, before screaming, "look out!" Of course, it was too late, we didn't have a chance to react before the man pushed his way to the door. Obviously Russian, he wore a neatly pressed Russian officer's military uniform. But it said Soviet Union on the insignia embroidered on the sleeve of his jacket. This didn't make any sense either, considering the Soviet Union fell years ago. I thought maybe someone hadn't sent this guy the memo, that was until six more Russian soldiers with the same uniform stormed the building.

Smoking a cigarette, the high-ranking Russian man walked over to a chair that Eric had been sitting in just minutes earlier and spun it around, taking a seat.

"Well," he started off, in a heavy Russian accent, "you have become, somewhat of a thorn in my side Ms. Elkin. I can only assume; these must be your children. Let me guess, the girl she specializes in martial arts, and knows more languages than God himself.

The boy, he is an intellectual genius, that reads quantum theory physics books for bedtime stories, is highly gifted at understanding plasma and its positive and negative energies. Although you, my dear woman. You confuse the KGB, why would a seemingly normal stay-at-home mother and a housewife want to be a spy? This is a question that has perplexed my comrades and I for many months. Do you care to explain, mind you it will not save your life? Still, it would be nice to know."

"I thought the Soviet Union collapsed? Why are you wearing Soviet era uniforms, trying to resurrect the dead? Whatever your planning, you won't get away with it. There are so many federal agencies crawling up my butt, I can hardly sit down. You can't honestly believe you can escape all of them."

The man smiled, flashing his two front gold teeth and let out a maniacal chuckle. "Come now Ms. Elkin you underestimate me. What makes you think that those agencies aren't linked to this. You think you're holier than thou Western government will ever tell you the truth? Your culture is like a cancer on the human race. You consume every natural resource, and then move on to the next, leaving nothing but death and destruction in your wake."

"The United States of America, is the greatest damn country in the world. Don't you ever forget it. You never heard about Americans defecting to Russia."

"Oh, I beg to differ. What about your Mr. Snowden because if I recollect, he was one of your top spies? Guess where he lives now Ms. Elkin. Not in Orlando Florida," the man said, his hot smelly breath filling our nasal cavities as his shoes made a scuffing sound on the wet pavement.

The Russian-made Sikorsky 880-M attack helicopter lifted off with a plume of snow that appeared to be smoke from a distance. Rising higher into the sky, the aircraft worked back before finding its way forward. The Russian soldiers sat across from us, their guns trained on our chests.

I was afraid to say anything, so I sat quietly, holding Emma in my lap. I looked out the window, but couldn't see very much, the blinding snow relentlessly pummeled the helicopter windows as we plowed through it.

We had been in the air for almost three hours, by my calculations. I knew the machine was too small to hold the fuel to get us into Russian territory, so I wondered what their next plan of attack would be and if it would consist of us being killed. Then I thought about his comment regarding Edward Snowden. I didn't know much about him; except re-released classified files he had discovered while working as a programmer for the Pentagon.

Of course, it was a breach of national security. And once it was discovered he had leaked classified documents, he was immediately terminated from this position and stripped of his security clearance. Eventually, he was brought up on charges of treason but fled the country before they could stick. So, he was not only a spy, he was also a traitor and someone who I'd consider to be as trustworthy and dangerous.

"Ms. Elkin," the Russian man's voice penetrated my helmet they had fastened to me before lift-off. "Please, be reasonable all we want is the map. If you give it to us, we will let you and your children go. No fuss, no muss. Very easy, you see, why must there be so much tension between you and I, we both have jobs to do. Of course, mine is a loving country that I would die for and yours is nothing but a bloated pig."

"I hope I'm alive when our government hangs you from a flagpole at Guantánamo Bay. I hear the waterboarding is much nicer in the spring."

"Search her for the map, check the children too, I know they must have it. They wouldn't be out here if they didn't find it!" Although after searching all three of us, they came up empty. I was sure we had both pieces of it, I just didn't know where, and considering our close quarters, asking Eric or Emma was out of the question.

The whirling blades of the helicopter made it hard to think, chopping through the ice-cold air just outside the metal shell. Eventually, a mountain range came into view. But it wasn't Alps, so I asked Eric, with a point of my finger.

"If I had to guess, I'd say Southwest Poland."

Why would we be in Poland? I didn't think Russians and Polish people got along. But there were a lot of things I was learning on this trip. Of course, most of them I could've done without.

"Are we there yet?" Emma asked, making me smile.

"No," one of the soldiers said in a stern tone, "and please sit down. If we hit turbulence, you could be hurt."

Emma followed the soldier's instructions, and sat back down, but not before sticking her tongue out at him. Although he didn't seem like the others, I noticed this earlier when he refused to point his weapons at the kids. Even when his fellow comrades did, I wondered if he wanted to defect. What reinforced this belief, was when he leaned his head back, and gave me a wink. I thought to myself, what if he's just doing that because he thinks I'm cute?

Eric pressed his face up against the oval shaped plexiglass, and stared out at the mountains that we were coming dangerously close to. "That's Owl Mountain, I recognize it from the maps."

"We're in Poland, seriously?"

"It's just on the other side of Germany Mom. They have trains that run back and forth through Germany and France every day."

The giant turbines above our hubs, started to slow the rotation as we descended. Since Eric recognized the terrain, I wasn't too concerned. That was until, three large armor-plated vehicles pulled up to meet the chopper at touchdown and a half a dozen more men jumped out, all heavily armed. Within just a few hundred feet from the mouth of the cave, I could see an army of men excavating from an area opposite from the public.

They had an excavator, and a bulldozer along with 10 train cars that disappeared into the forest. The large helicopter door swung open with a bang, and we were ordered outside into the snow. At first, I was afraid we were to be executed, then a man drove up in a Jeep that was equipped with rubber tracks on the back two wheels.

"The general will see you now," the driver announced. After helping us into the cover, we were sped off to a location just a few hundred feet from the base of the mountain to what appeared to be a small trailer with just two windows on its side.

We walked in, and were told to sit down in the chairs placed in front of us. Not knowing what to expect, I instructed the kids to keep their mouths shut and their ears open, and to not say anything unless there was no other options.

Sitting there waiting, was torture itself because once again, it gave my brain time to run rampant. Thinking about all the worst-case scenarios, I was working myself up into a frenzy. Until Emma kicked my foot with her boot and pulled me out of the trance. We could hear voices coming from the room that was adjacent to the one we were sitting in but couldn't understand what they were saying. Although we could deduct it was in Russian.

The closed-door to the room the noises emanated from burst open. A portly man donning the Russian officer's uniform, stepped out, and checked his collar before approaching us.

"My name is Gen. Reinhardt. I believe you have something that belongs to me," the almost bald man said, pushing his gold rimmed glasses back to the bridge of his nose.

Not knowing how to respond, I sat silent and glared at the kids. But I could tell he didn't believe me, and that something bad was going to happen soon. However, I kept dwelling on the fact that the 'good guys always win,' and I thought we were the good guys. Although considering where we were sitting currently, I had to wonder.

The Gen. walked around us, tilting his head from side to side, like he was examining us. He pointed at Eric, and yelled something. But it sounded more like German than Russian. It was all starting to make sense; all of these guys were German hangers on of the third right. That's why they were Russian uniforms, but spoke in German. They were Nazis. It all made sense. They were trying to steal the gold back from the guys who originally put it there. Of course, the more I thought about it, the more ridiculous it was that the CIA thought we were ready for something like this.

Suddenly, there was a large explosion, it was followed by a gigantic plume of rock and dust blowing out of the entrance where the workers had been digging. Men ran around frantically, trying to sift through the chaos and debris. It appeared they had an explosion they had not predicted.

The raging storm that had been following us, finally caught up. The howling winds, nipped at the trailer door. A man dressed all in black, came out of the back room of the trailer holding a black 1960s Dr. bag. Opening it up, he pulled out a syringe and clicked it two times with his finger.

With a thick German accent, he said, "This is flunitrazepam."

I recognized the name. Flunitrazepam, also known as Rohypnol among other names, is a benzodiazepine used to treat severe insomnia and assist with anesthesia. As with other hypnotics, flunitrazepam has been advised to be prescribed only on a short-term basis or by those with chronic insomnia on an occasional basis. However, it's more recent use, has been as a true serum, of course, but also causes psychotic episodes and outbreaks of violence if overused.

"What you plan on doing with that?" I asked, knowing full well his intentions.

"We know you have the map. Give it to me, and no one gets hurt. The more you resist, the worse it will get. I come from a long line of people who have a gift for getting the truth. So, what is it going to be?" he said, again clicking the syringe filled with a yellow liquid.

Chapter Sixteen

"Kiss my butt, we're not telling you crap," Emma said, flicking her hair back.

Let me just say, I was not happy with my daughter's choice of language. But it was appropriate, considering the circumstance. So, I let it ride, I figured why the hell not. What's the worst that could happen, at this point?

"Very well, have it your way," the man dressed in black, with dark glasses said, approaching Emma first.

Two other men came from the back room that the man with a doctor's bag and the general had come from. They restrained Emma as the creepy wannabe physician grabbed her forearm and inserted the needle. Methodically, he injected all three of us with the flunitrazepam. At some point, they let us back down the stairs and outside into the snow.

The howling wind bit at the tips of our fingers as the snow cascaded around us like trying to build a cocoon. But the rest of my body wasn't cold, as a matter of fact, it was warm. I assumed a side effect of the drug that was running through our veins. My mouth was dry. However, as I tried to lick my lips and moisten my palate, I couldn't muster enough saliva to do so. It was like the medication was dehydrating us.

Emma collapsed into the snow, but was quickly scooped up by one of the men and thrown over his shoulder like a bag of potatoes. I could barely see, but I could tell Eric wasn't faring much better. His legs were weak, wobbling every couple of feet, so I knew it wouldn't be long before he went down as well.

Repeating the phrase, 'stay awake' every couple of seconds in my head, I thought was assisting me. But before I knew it, the ground looked closer until my face hit the cold snow-covered ground. Even with my eyes shut, I felt my body jerked off the ground. I assumed I was also picked up. Bouncing on another man's shoulders, my body was limp, but my eyes were open. I could just barely make out a large cylindrical silver-looking object in front of us. Sounds of airplane engines filled my ears, before I finally passed out completely.

I'm not sure how long we were unconscious. But when we woke up, we found our hands and feet tied to a silver bench that was fastened to the wall. I struggled for a moment, trying to free my hands but it was no use. They were bound tightly. I noticed Emma, and Eric waking up and tried to get their attention. But their bodies were not absorbing the drug as well as mine. So, it took them a little longer to regain their bearings and come to their senses.

There were oval windows lining each side of the room. At first when I glanced out through the one directly beside me, I thought I had seen clouds but I convinced myself I was hallucinating because of the drugs. So, I turned my attention back to Emma who was closer to me. Finally, but still in a groggy haze, she looked up at me before trying to brush the hair from her face.

"Why are our hands tied?" she said, snapping her wrist up, trying to break the lashings that secured us.

However, none of the people in view replied. Preoccupied with something else. they stayed focused on what they were doing, ignoring us entirely. The medication must've affected out hearing because it took me a few moments before the sound outside the window caught my hearing. It was the sound I had heard before passing out. Airplane engines. But the interior didn't resemble an airplane. At least not any that I'd ever been in before, so I was unsure of our location.

After another few minutes had passed, Eric lifted his head. He made eye contact with me first, then his sister. He looked around the room we were in, but appeared perplexed. Shaking his head a few times, he tried to clear it. He looked around again and then back at me like he was expecting answers, but I had none.

"Where are we?" he said, "God, my head hurts so bad. Did I fall or something?"

However, I had a headache and I was sure Emma did also. Looking around the room, I looked for any distinguishable marks that would give us an idea of where we currently were. But there wasn't anything. At least nothing minus a fire extinguisher that hung on the wall next to a door.

"I think we're in a blimp," Eric said, leaning his head back against the wall.

"A blimp? Why are we in a blimp? Mom, what the heck is going on?" Emma said, chiming in.

But I didn't know, and I sure didn't want to acknowledge it. The soldier that had refused to train his weapon on the kids sitting just to the left of us. I noticed him with his head leaning back against the wall and his eyes closed. So, I made eye contact with Emma in hopes of getting her attention. Although she didn't understand what I wanted.

So, I whispered, "Ask him a question."

After beckoning for his attention for a couple of minutes, he finally opened his eyes and glared at Emma but didn't say anything at first. He looked at Eric, and then me "What, do you want?" he asked.

"Excuse me," I said, "where are we?"

"On our way to Berlin," he said, turning his attention to the window beside his elbow.

"Why, what's in Germany?" Emma asked, hoping for a reply.

Not sure if we would get an answer. The ambience of the cabin grew stagnant with the mind-numbing stress as we waited for his response. Eventually turning his head, he stared at Emma for a moment. Then looking over at Eric and then back to me, he said, "That is where our headquarters are located. You should not have come. Just know when we land, you're of no use to us, and if you don't have the map, then, there would be no reason to keep you alive. Do you understand," he said with an expressionless face?

"Can I have my backpack, please?" Emma bravely asked.

"I suppose so, but if you try anything little girl. It will not end well, do you understand me," he said reaching above his head and opening a bin.

Pulling the satchel from the compartment, it dropped into his lap. Closing the bin door, he set the backpack across Emma's legs and then reached behind her back and untied one of her restraints. He stared at the bag for a moment. "Your bag, it resembles a parachute. See them stacked against the wall, right over there. You better keep track of this, if there is an accident, someone could mistake it for a functioning chute. They would have a very bad surprise."

Emma used her free hand and opened her bag. Reaching to the very bottom, she found what she was looking for. Her last piece of gum. Holding the wrapper between her teeth, she unfurled it. She rested the chunk of watermelon flavored bubble gum on her tongue before wadding the piece of paper up and discarding it back in the bag.

"Are you going to kill us? I'm young, so I don't care you can tell me."

Emma's question caught the man off-guard. He'd never had such a direct question asked by a child before. He wasn't sure how to respond. He stared at her for a minute. "Why would you say such a thing? I just have a job to do. It is not my problem if you are a child or not. But I am not a heartless bastard, I have a daughter myself. Strangely, she is about your age," he acknowledged, opening a long wallet he'd pulled from the inside pocket of his uniform. "See, she has blonde hair too, just like you. You and her, you could be sisters."

He closed his wallet, and positioned it back in its original resting place. Turning his attention to the cockpit of the aircraft, he stood up and walked towards the pilot area before looking back at Emma and I. However, before he walked out of sight, I swore he winked at me. But I had to be sure, this wasn't a situation I could afford to be wrong about. I whispered to Emma, "I think you got through to him."

"Hey, M try to do some cute kid things. It'll make him think about his kid, and screw with his head. It's our only chance M."

Now I was sure the man had winked at me, giving me some sign, he was on our side. I just prayed I wasn't wrong because I had misread things before. Of course, nothing like this, but the more I thought about it, I was sure he winked at me. Based on this, I whispered my plan to Eric. He agreed, and instructed his sister.

There was a noise in the cockpit. It sounded like struggle. We could feel the aircraft shake back and forth, from side to side, like something substantial was causing the shift. Then it dawned on me, Emma's hand was still free, the man never retied it. I couldn't believe, it was so obvious, the whole time right in front of me. But the drugs were just now starting to wear off completely, to where I felt halfway normal again. So, I didn't beat myself up too much as Emma untied us.

"Well, well," the general's voice resonated. "Going somewhere? My dear woman, look outside. We are 15,000 feet in the air. So, be my guest the door is right over there."

I bit down on my lip and looked at the kids. However, Emma was always a firecracker and you never knew when she's gonna blow. And before I knew it, the general was hunched over on the floor gasping for air. Emma had kicked him in the groin, which of course, didn't surprise me in the slightest. "That a girl, M! Kick his butt," Eric yelled, causing the other men from the back room to flood the cabin.

A fight ensued, and since my shoulder wasn't back up to standards. I reached over and grabbed the fire extinguisher from its holster. I raised it high above my head, cracking the general on the skull. I pulled the pin and sprayed the contents in the face of the first two men that made it through the doorway. Realizing it was causing more harm than good, I let go of the trigger and use the cylinder as a blunt object, knocking out two more soldiers before we had regained control of the area.

Crossing my arms in self-satisfaction, I congratulated myself too soon because I heard a click of a gun. Someone was behind me with the barrel of a weapon pressed up against my back. I couldn't see who it was, but I noticed the general was no longer on the floor in front of us. So that gave me a good idea who was holding the gun.

"You're not gonna get out of this general. One way or another. Give up now, and we won't kill you. But if you fight, all bets are off," I said, trying to act tough, but inside a trembling circus.

Suddenly out of the cockpit, our would be here arrived. "TO THE RIGHT," he yelled, lining his weapon up with my chest. I took heed to his warning, and took a dive towards the right-hand side of the cabin. Before I landed, I heard two shots, "PEWWW, BANG!" Then nothing, no sounds or voices. I was afraid to open my eyes as I laid on the ground huddled next to a bag. However, before we could regain our senses, the aircraft leaned sharply to the left, then back to the right again, appearing it was out of control, or a pilotless.

But like as if it was a sign from the universe, the blimp leveled off and appeared to be back at a normal elevation. The sound of rushing air, filled the cabin, sucking out random debris that was scattered around the floors. The table had overturned and knocked the stack of parachutes that a been piled in a storage container all over the floor. The sound of the rushing wind grew louder, as my eyes adjusted, I could see why. The general had pushed a button on the wall for the ramp. It was opening.

Feeling the bitter cold air on our faces and exposed limbs, sent a chill down our spines. I tried to stand but my balance still hadn't returned completely, so I had to utilize the wall for balance so I wouldn't fall over. However, as I looked down, our hero didn't fare as well. He had been shot. Even though the injury looked minor, only striking his shoulder midway up, I knew he could bleed to death in a very short time if we didn't pack the wound.

The general staggered to his feet, clicking his empty gun at Emma first and then I and Eric. Frustrated, he pulled a small two shot derringer handgun from his pocket and searched the floor for a parachute. Holding us at bay with a small firearm, he slid his arms through the straps, they clicked the waist belt snug.

The ramp now completely extended exposed the outside world in its entirety. The chilled air acted as a vacuum sucking everything out not nailed down. I grabbed Emma and held on to her with all my might while pushing back against Eric so they wouldn't meet an untimely demise. Though the general had other ideas, I heard the first shot land in the wall next to my ear. The second one, however, found its mark and lodged itself in my abdomen.

At first, I wasn't even aware I had been shot. That was until the ungodly burning started. It felt like someone had a red-hot fire poker and was jabbing me in the stomach with it. Try not to look down at my wound, fearing it would do no good, I turned my attention back to the general because I heard Eric say, "His gun's empty mom, that's only a two shot."

Of course, by now, he had managed his way back towards the entrance of the ramp. Glaring back at the three of us, saying, "This isn't over. I will return, and when I do, I will make sure to kill you slowly," then jumping out the waiting entrance.

"HEY! Where's my backpack?" squealed Emma.

Our German ally sat up then. "I think the general needed it more than you, young one."

I had a bad habit, of taking a sigh of relief prematurely.

This was one of those times because I realized even with the general gone, our problems had just begun. I didn't know how to fly a blimp, that I was sure of, and I was also sure there wasn't a radio controller that would teach me. I looked at Eric but didn't even want to ask if he knew how, both of them had been through way too much to ask them to assist on anything else.

Before I started to freak out, I figured I'd better check my wound. Even though the reality of it was, I didn't want to. I was afraid to see how bad the injury was. However, to my relief the bullet had lodged itself into the handle of my 'S.P.O.T.' device. So, I turned my attention to the chaos unfolding in front of me.

"My name is Hans Berge," our new German friend announced. Eric helped Hans off the floor and up onto the bench. While Emma examined the man's wound, I adjourned to the cockpit and looked around for anything that would instruct us on how to land. The craft now aimlessly drifting in the breeze, had no engines.

However, as I had seen in movies years earlier, about the Hindenburg, I remembered them turning a series of knobs. So, I knew it had to consist of a valve, of some sort that would help deflate the craft. I also knew that a blimp was very similar to a hot air balloon and that we had to use caution. We didn't want it to deflate too quickly. We'd drop out of the sky like a brick if we did.

I rubbed my temples in a circular pattern for a couple of seconds. There appeared to be more gauges, knobs and buttons in this cockpit than the jumbo jet I had landed earlier. Which personally, I felt was overkill and made zero sense, but I didn't work for Goodyear, so it wasn't my call. Not to mention, everything was in German.

"Where the hell, did that come from?" I yelled, after glancing out the cockpit window and seeing a giant mountain coming directly at us.

"I so didn't sign up for this crap," I mumbled, heading back into the cabin.

"We've got a big problem," I said, grabbing Hans by his good arm and leading him into the cockpit, "that!"

He stared at the mountainous mass for a second before sitting down in the pilot seat. Gripping the controls, he attempted to turn the craft, but appeared to be having difficulties. "They locked the steering; I can't turn it. It feels like the rudder is frozen or something."

"How are we supposed to get out of here?" I said in a panic, not hearing how hysterical I actually sounded until Eric alerted me to calm down.

I won't lie, I was so frazzled I couldn't see straight. I hadn't gotten a good night's sleep in over a week. I'd been shot, attacked by a bear and skied off the side of a mountain. I was so done with this; it wasn't even funny. I longed for my boring life after this. I'll take ironing and dirty clothes over this any day.

About 15 minutes had passed. Everything was quiet, too quiet, there should've been some type of noise, but I think everyone was so freaked out, nobody knew what to say. So we sat there silent in the cockpit, looking at each other. Eventually, the silence was broken by Emma. "You know there's a plane underneath this thing?"

"Really?" I said.

Chapter Seventeen

"She is correct. I had forgotten about it. It hangs under the blimp. It's in case were attacked. But I'm afraid there're only two seats. I don't know if it would do us any good."

Making our way to the belly of the aircraft, I looked through the viewport down at the plane. I could see the cockpit. Hans was right, there were only two seats. So, I resigned myself to staying on board and letting Eric and Emma go. It was the right thing to do. But Hans had a better idea, after his explanation, I had a little hope, we probably all would survive. But I didn't have a lucky rabbit's foot, so all I could do was cross my fingers and hope that Hans could figure out a way to make this work.

I was fresh out of ideas, I had nothing left, I had given everything and then some. However, if my kids are involved, I would take one for the team. I didn't want to die, but I wasn't gonna let my children die either. Even if it meant sacrificing myself, then so be it. I didn't believe I felt any different than any other parent because their bond with their children is unbreakable. So, while I had the time, I hugged Eric and Emma tightly and kissed their dirty hair, telling them how much I loved them and appreciated the time we had together.

During my farewell speech, Hans pulled me aside. He explained he would go down in the pilot seat first, and I would hand Emma down that way she would sit on his lap. Then I would crawl down into the backseat, and Eric would sit in my lap. He said it was the only way, the only way we would have a chance of surviving because if we stayed on the craft much longer, we would surely meet our end.

Hans pulled the handle back on the viewport door. Turning the large bolt that held the door closed, the door opened up and landed against the wall behind it with a loud "THUD!"

He grabbed a hold of the steps and lowered himself down into the cockpit of the bi-plane. The wind was strong, almost knocking him out of the plane twice. Finally, he managed to get to the seat and pulled himself down, planting the seat belt around his waist and clamping it shut.

Just a howling wind could be heard as the engines on the inflatable aircraft, it ceased working earlier on in the flight, until a low roaming rumble echoed from the front of the plane and wisps of smoke erupted. Suddenly, the blimp shuddered, and its nose pointed straight towards the mountain.

One thing bothered me though, I knew the small attack aircraft like the one under the blimp. They had a weight capacity, generally consisting of only around 300 to 400 pounds. If my calculations were correct, all four of us would be too much, we'd be too heavy. My mind raced a mile a minute, I couldn't figure out what to do.

The only plan in my head, again doomed me to reside in the blimp. I estimated Hans weighed 200, that meant the plane could only take one more adult or in this case two children. I assured myself I wouldn't be one of them.

Eric looked up at me, but I shook my head. "I love you very much, and I'm so proud of you. You and your sister have exceeded my expectations beyond leaps and bounds. I want you to look after your sister because she's going to need you. And don't ever forget how much I love you. Now get down there, and go save the world."

He wrapped his arms around my waist, and squeezed me tighter than he ever had, declaring how much he would miss me. I made him promise me, he would never tell his sister because even though Emma had turned into a badass, she was still my little girl. And I knew this would not be easy on her, and she would need extra help.

I made eye contact with Hans and shook my head. He understood, as I'm sure he was well aware of the weight restrictions. I watched my daughter, for what I thought would be the last time, fumble with the controls on the dashboard of the plane. I could only assume; she was questioning Hans about everyone and their function. I waited until Eric crawled into the backseat, it secured a seatbelt before I closed the hatch and watched the plane fall from the belly of the blimp.

I sank down hard on the bench we had been secured to at the beginning of the flight and started to cry. I thought about my father and mother, my dog Rosie and how much I would miss them all. But in a strange way, I felt a sign of accomplishment, knowing that my children would live because of my sacrifice. However, as I sat there, lighting the candles on the cake at my own pity party.

Wiping the tears back from my eyes, I noticed the waiting pile of parachutes laying on the floor. But I'd counted a total of eight when I recovered from the truth serum. I now understood what Hans was referring to when he told Emma the general had needed her backpack more. The jackass thought her backpack was one of the parachutes. So, I guess he wouldn't be back after all.

Spinning around, I looked up the cockpit window, I could see how close the mountain was. So, without a minute to spare, I bent down and grabbed one of the parachutes, making sure it was real, I strapped it to my back and buckled the straps around my waist and chest. I walked to the ramp, and looked down at the mountain range passing underneath the aircraft. I figured, there was no time like the present. I walked down the ramp, until my shoes near splitting and I slid off the back out into the open expanse. The wind grabbed me immediately and jerked me backwards.

I pulled the ripcord. The white and orange shoot billowed from its housing, scooping up the air as it went. Opening up with a loud pop, the design did its job and arrested my fall. Although now, I had a new set of problems. I was out in some below temperatures with nothing more than a sweatshirt, a pair of blue jeans and a pair of timberland hiking boots. The winter wind blew me around like a pendulum on a string, slinging me from side to side with every gust. However, through all of this, I was able to gain a glimpse of the kids plane as it was still flying along the rocky crevasse.

I guess I must've passed out because the next thing I knew, something sharp hit my cheek and caused me to wake up. I opened my eyes and examined my surroundings. I had landed on a shelf about 200 feet off the ground. One thing that I did notice, however, was the smoke streaming from the wreckage of the blimp that was just off to my right, a few thousand feet away and the occasional explosions that emanated from it.

Trying to assure myself I would be okay, I sat up and removed my harness, fearing the parachute would catch more wind and blow me off the side of the cliff. There was a small 20- or 25-inch opening in the cave. Generally, I was claustrophobic, but in this case, I felt if I didn't get shelter soon, I wouldn't survive very long. But I kept my wits about me, and made sure I had nothing that would obstruct, or cause me to get stuck in the hole before I crawled in. Of course, the first thing I noticed was the rancid odor of rotting meat.

I concluded this was a bear's den. But I didn't see the animal and presumed he was nowhere to be found. At first getting out of the wind seemed to be enough, to help take the chill off. But eventually, my teeth began to chatter, as I could see my breath in the air in front of me. And whether it was psychosomatic or not, I had to gain more warmth.

 I looked around to see if there was anything, I could use to start a fire and saw two sticks and a rock sitting in the back off next to a dried-out pile of thickets.

Remembering my Girl Scout training, I positioned the rock under the dead thickets, then worked the two sticks in between the palm of my hands, spinning them as fast as I could in order to cause friction. To my surprise, a tiny cloud of smoke erupted before one orange flame popped up, followed by another and then another. But my hands were now cut and bleeding. So, I stuck them in some random snow sitting by my leg. Which for a moment felt pretty good, until I started thinking about all of the bacteria there must be in it from being around a large predator such as a bear.

I was exhausted. I could barely see because of the blistering wind that slammed into my face. My stomach was rumbling with hunger pains, and I was sure two of my ribs, possibly three had been broken in the landing. Trying to pay no mind to the multiple problems that plagued me, I thought about Emma and Eric and prayed they would land safe. Of course, immediately thereafter, I thought of the reason I had to worry about their safety. That general. I always taught my children to live and let live. But the hatred I had for that man was enough to fill a football stadium three times over. I was glad he got what he had coming.

That didn't make my situation any easier to accept, however, as I felt like I'd been run over by a dump truck. After the fire was going, to the point where I felt it wouldn't go out, I laid my head back on the dirt floor of the cave. I tried to steady my breathing, but it was hard. I didn't know if I should cry or be elated, I'd survived what I had assumed would be my end.

I began to dream that I was home sitting on the beach. Eric was playing in the water, while Emma was looking at a seashell down by the shoreline. There was a warm breeze coming off the water that encased us in the circle of comfort. The seagulls squawked in the background, while the crash of the waves drowned out some of their cries.

Then Eric called my name, and then again and again. But his calls were still in my head as my eyes opened. At first, I thought I might had been asleep, but then I heard the cries again. This time they appeared to be right outside. But I didn't trust my state of mind. My brain had played tricks on me before, I remembered I was at least a couple hundred feet off the ground. So, I stayed put and eventually fell back asleep. The next time I awoke, it was dark outside, and no sunlight was visible. I could hear what I thought was a helicopter.

I cautiously crawled to the entrance of the cave and hesitated at first before sticking my head out. It was amazing how quickly you'd become paranoid, being a spy. Multiple searchlights panned the area, brightening up the landscape like the sun. Large round wide beams of light penetrated the rocky canopy and outcrop of mountains. Unfortunately, I didn't know if the people operating them were friend or foe. So, I figured my best bet was to stay silent and not alert them to my location.

However, as I began a backwards crawl into the cave. I heard my name, "BRENDA ELKIN, THIS IS THE CIA. CAN YOU HEAR US?"

"Oh my God! I"M OVER HERE! OVER HERE!" I screamed, getting to my feet outside of the entrance of the cave. I waved my arms over my head, but realizing they couldn't see me due to the darkness; I slid through the cave entrance and grabbed a handful of burning thickets from the makeshift campfire and waved them in the air.

The blinding light swung from across the other side of the crevasse and landed on me, illuminating my spot like the sun had exploded. Within just a couple of minutes, I heard more voices off to my right and then my left, but to my relief they were all speaking English because frankly, I was more than happy to just stick with one language, my native one.

Like a behemoth rising from the grave, a Black Hawk helicopter came within just a few feet of me, and hit me with its jet wash from its rotors, but the insignia on the side of the chopper was an American flag. They helped me inside as the medics tended to my wounds and shoulder which had been killing me since I'd left the hospital in Switzerland.

"I'm major McDaniel's, you're safe."

At first, I couldn't understand how they found me, then I remembered the Gen.'s bullet had landed in the handle of the 'S.P.O.T.' location system. It must've caused the device to go off inadvertently, and tagged me. The damn general saved my life, and didn't even know it.

"I gotta send him a Christmas card," I laughed, before resting my head on the gurney.

After getting released from the hospital in Berlin, I was more than ready to get home. But the kids convinced me to go see the monument at Owl Mountain. It was dedicated to the men and women who died while tunneling for the Nazis during World War II. I found it strange at first that either one of them took interest in this, not because they're not empathetic or sympathetic to the tragedies of that time. Simply because they were always more engrossed in electronics and video games.

The CIA, kindly give us a ride. So, we were there at the base of the mountains in no time. All of the general's equipment had been removed, and the area had been cordoned off and was now armed with Polish soldiers from the Polish military. They were firm in their demands of keeping them back, away from the boundaries, as it had already had one disaster, the explosion. They determined it was caused by built-up carbon monoxide and carbon dioxide gas under the mountain.

Experts said it'd been trapped there since the tunnels were built almost 70 years earlier. It was only ignited, by the constant bombardment of blasting caps and long diamond tipped drill bits that tore through the soil clipping rocks and other minerals along the way, which in turn caused a spark.

"Mom...," Eric said, crouching down to keep his silhouette out of sight through the fading daylight.

He grabbed Emma by the hand and dragged her with him, running through the frozen snow, we made it to the south side of Owl Mountain. I watched our chopper pilots talking to the Polish soldiers because even though he didn't know what our plan was, inadvertently he was sure helping it succeed.

However, Eric stopped. He pointed to a spot on the ground before he began digging, pushing handfuls of dirt aside, Emma joined in and lent him a hand. By the time they finished, daylight was completely gone. The only thing we had available were penlight flashlights for our means of illumination. Eric wouldn't quit, don't get me wrong he's normally a tenacious teenager, but this was unusual, even for him, and Emma wasn't faring much better.

"I found it. I found the entrance," Eric announced, putting the tiny flashlight back between his teeth.

The hair on the back of my neck stood up when I heard his announcement because I didn't mind being poor, it wasn't like we went without. We had a nice home, good food to eat, warm clothes to wear. Don't get me wrong, we didn't drive a Mercedes either, but we were comfortable, however, just the thought of that reward money made me drool. I would've been happy with $10,000, but millions, I couldn't even imagine what I would do if I have that type of money.

Eric climbed down the tunnel first, he helped to sister and then me. The stench of mildew, and stagnant water was everywhere and the drips of free-flowing water hitting the ground could be heard all around us. We started to walk down the tunnel, until Eric pointed his penlight at a sign on the wall. It was in German, it translated to hail Hitler. I instantly grew nauseous and felt sick to my stomach, knowing that such a person had walked on the ground under my feet.

We walked for a few hundred feet more until Eric stopped. He dropped his light, and Emma didn't speak a word.

Rather than asking them what the problem was, I walked up to the spot they had stopped in. It was then that I saw what made them stop in their tracks. A giant locomotive, with a coal car still filled to the top attached behind it, and behind that, covered train cars. I wasn't not sure how many, just a lot. I placed my hand on Eric shoulder and said, "You found it. By God you found it."

"So, what do we do now?" Emma said, taking a few steps closer to the train.

Eric didn't say anything, he was still in shock. Basically, because I don't think he thought it was real, and frankly neither did I. But it was kind of hard to deny its existence, especially when it was less than 50 feet from us. But this entire trip had been hard to swallow, from the time we left Florida until now. "Eric? You okay son?" I asked.

Finally, he turned around, tears streaming down his face. "It's real! It's real Mom! And I found it!" he exclaimed.

However, as the excitement and jubilation filled our souls, Eric grabbed Emma by the arm and yanked her backwards. "What do you think you're doing?"

"There is more than enough butthead. Mom. Tell Eric to share!"

"What's wrong Eric?" I said concerned there was something we had missed."

"They set booby-traps. I'm sure of it. If we set one of them off, they all could go off and cave in the ceiling."

"Trapped like rats, leave it to the Nazis. So, what do we do?" I said, pulling them both back closer to me.

"Nothing."

"What... You've got to be out of your mind. You dragged us all the way through hell and back, and now you don't want to take any of the spoils. Mom, can you please talk some sense into your son, I think his elevator stopped going to the top floor."

Chapter Eighteen

"Emma, stop it. Your brother knows what he's talking about, he's gotten us this far, give him a little credit. Eric, look at me. Are you sure?"

"Yes, look right there, do you see that monofilament line. It's fishing line, why would it be draped from one side of the cave to the other?" he said, pointing his light at it.

"Well, there goes our payday. I guess... I guess we go home now."

"WHAT? Are you insane, it's right there Mom!"

"Emma, keep your voice down, do you know how sensitive these explosives are after being down here so long. You could set one off," Eric snapped.

"Your brother's right, and don't talk to me like that young lady. I can still ground you, you know, don't forget that. Now, if your brother says it's dangerous, it's dangerous. End of story. Let's go," I said, giving the train one last look, so I could try and remember it and dream about its riches in my sleep.

"Do you think we should tell anyone?" Eric asked.

"That's up to you honey, it's your discovery."

"Why would you even want to, they can't take anything," Emma said, with heavy sarcasm.

I crawled out of the tunnel first. Then helped Emma out. Eric stood below her, making sure if she fell, she'd be caught. Once we were all on the surface, I caught the attention of our pilot. I waved at him, and spun my hand above my head as a gesture to start the engines.

Looking back at the mountain, I realized it was my secret and one I'd take to my grave.

The End?